SANSA &
THE LONELY TROLL

Written and Illustrated by
Samantha Buckley

THE CHILDREN OF THE *AOS SI* : BOOK ONE

Terran Empire Publishing
1761 Hillside Ct
Placerville, CA 95667

Date of Publication: April, 2018

ISBN 978-0-9992022-1-0

SPECIAL THANKS TO THE FOLLOWING MUSES WHO INSPIRED THIS STORY:

SANSA

REX

RIN

ROBERT

PATRICIA

MATT

GENA

NADINE

NEIL

There are fables and legends about magical beings and other realms; of creatures that roamed the land, Fae kings and queens that ruled the realms, hidden away from the rest of us. There are stories of different portals that used to lead to magical lands but have since disappeared-if they ever existed at all.

The Fae were known for wielding magic; communing with animals, nature, and the elements; and for either helping or causing mischief for the humans. Many centuries ago, a battle broke out between branches of the Fae, dividing them into two distinct factions: the Dark and the Light. Although they had ongoing skirmishes and raids, they soon found that they had a common enemy: humans.

The humans were jealous of their kind, as well as their connection to the magical world around them. After the largest, most devastating battle between the Fae Realms and the human one, the doorways to the Fae Realms had been thought sealed, and no Fae creatures have been seen since.

Or so we believed....

THE FIRE CRACKLED softly, light shimmering around the small clearing as shadows danced over the surrounding trees and bushes. The sound of water falling could be heard over the quiet crackle of the campfire. Nearby, two large trees created an archway that seemed to sparkle in the flickering light. The moon was shining down, full and bright in the dark sky. It was nearing dawn and stars had begun to fade in preparation for the morning sun.

A large figure huddled close to the small fire, trying to keep warm while keeping the light low enough that they wouldn't be seen in the dark woods and quiet night. The flames seemed to flare for a moment as a small flicker of light stepped out of the low pyre and approached the stooped creature. The troll looked down at his small friend, thankful that Lasair, his family's most trusted Hearth Fae and his constant companion, had decided to join him on this journey into the unknown.

The friends were tired. They had been traveling all day, moving as quietly and covertly as possible. They had avoided the main roads, villages, and inns, moving towards *An Tuar Ceatha* and the portal that rested at the foot of the Rainbow Falls. King Aneirin had sent them to find the door to another realm - a world without Fae or magic. A world full of humans - those cruel creatures that hated, feared - and also desired - the powers and abilities of the Fae.

Between the Dark Fae and the humans, the Light Fae realm had been under siege for centuries. After thousands of Fae had been either killed or taken, the king had decided to make one final, desperate play. He was going to close the doorways to the human realm. Dark Fae travel would still be possible, but the humans were getting stronger and bolder.

Better to fight a war on one front, instead of two. The decision made sense, but it had one heartbreaking consequence for the king. It would prevent his daughter, Princess Maelona, from returning home.

She had left years ago, choosing a human male and a mortal life over her family, the Fae, and the throne. The king had let her leave, allowing her the freedom to pick love over duty. Unfortunately, this had more repercussions than could have been foreseen- beginning with the loss of morale, which lead to soldiers deserting their posts, less volunteers to help defend the realm, and an increase in missing Fae. The king's health had also started to decline as the blow to his heart had weakened his spirit, and he had begun to fall ill. The illness had decreased his strength and will, and the power it would take to close the portals would diminish him further.

Knowing his time was running out, King Aneirin had one last mission for his favorite guard and oldest friend. He was sending Tanrawdtatoeraswyn, Raswyn to his friends, to the human realm. He was to wait for the children of "*The Prophecy*" - children that were foretold by the Norn to unite the realms and stop the endless, bloody battles. The fate seers called them the children of the *Aos Si,* using the ancient term for the Fae races. Lasair had refused to allow Raswyn to go alone and had accompanied him on this lonely mission. Unfortunately, they had to travel quickly so as to make it before the King started the ritual. There was at least one spy in the castle, someone was feeding information to either the Dark Fae, the humans, but probably both.

This secret mission, along with the closing of the portals, was the final attempt to protect the weakening kingdom and the creatures that lived in the Light Fae Realm. The companions were taking one last rest in their home lands before braving the doorway to the human realm at dawn.

As the two sat next to the fire, contemplating their last night under the familiar sky, a loud crack resounded in the woods around them. Raswyn stood quickly, watching for any movement in the shadows. Lasair moved closer to the flames, preparing himself to protect Raswyn. As they stood, ready for whatever may have found them, dark figures stepped our of the trees around them. Raswyn squinted in the faint light, hoping he was wrong, hoping that these weren't creatures he had once called friends.

"What are you doing here, Raswyn?", the sly voice

carried over the still, night air. Raswyn recognized the voice and shook his head in disappointment. The speaker was another Royal Guard, a Gold Dragonkin by the name of Alwain. His golden scales glimmered in the fire light, and he was as tall as Raswyn, topping 7 feet. However, Alwain's eyes glinted with malice and jealousy as he sneered at the troll.

"Alwain! I'm on a Royal Mission to visit the mermaids that live near the falls. Did the king send you too? I told him that they no longer feared me...." Raswyn knew the only reason Alwain would be here was if there were darker forces at play. Hopefully the king still lived....

"You and I both know you are not visiting with the mermaids, Raswyn." Alwain looked at the troll with disdain, "The king sent you on a fool's errand. Why don't you tell me what it is you're looking for? I'm sure we would all love to help..." The creatures with Alwain snickered, knowing they would do no such thing.

They were clearly here to stop whatever plan the king had. However, their words also indicated that they had no idea what the plan was. That was all Raswyn needed to know. That meant there was still a chance. He and Lasair could still complete their mission, and they would. Raswyn looked over his shoulder and nodded at his friend, standing near the fire. He then turned back, facing the Dragonkin again. "I think we both know that you are not here to help. You have clearly changed your allegiance and care nothing for your king or our realm. Why not leave us to our business?" Raswyn had noticed the sky was lightening with the coming dawn. They were running out of time.

"That's why no one liked you, troll." Alwain sneered at Raswyn, "You were always so blinded by your faith to this weak king that you never saw how useless he is. That's about to change."

As Raswyn and Alwain were speaking, Lasair had begun to whisper softly. The small campfire started to pop and flare, as small flame creatures started to appear around the fire and Lasair. Lasair himself began to decrease in size, as every new flame creature drew some of his fire and magic. Ninety nine flame creatures arranged themselves around Lasair, preparing to defend the friends. They just waited for a sign of attack or a word from Lasair.

"Now, Lasair!" Raswyn called as he feinted towards Alwain, causing the Dragonkin to step back in surprise. Raswyn took advantage of his foe's surprise and turned, ready to grab Lasair as the other burning creatures made a large wall of flame between the troll and his now tiny friend. The flames reached ten feet into the night air, bathing the small clearing in a bright light. Raswyn bent over, scooping up the noticeably dimmed fire creature. He cupped his large hands, half covering the small creature who was fading in his arms. Turning, he ran towards the arched doorway to the other realm, trusting the flames to protect his back. Before he stepped into the now open portal, the troll stopped, looking back and calling quickly to the remaining flames. The wall of fire moved in unison to the portal, growing smaller before finally combining back into one small flame again, smaller than Lasair had been.

The two looked up, seeing the sky lighten with the coming dawn. Time was up. A keening could be heard, cutting through the sounds of the forest and the enemies closing in on the portal. King Aneirin had begun the ritual. They only had moments to get through before all doorways were closed. The creatures surrounding them, led by Alwain, continued to stalk closer, weapons drawn. As the two stepped into the doorway, the creatures charged forward, ready to follow them into the other realm. The first few threw themselves at the portal, only to charge through an empty space under the arched branches. They howled in anger and frustration, their cries drowning out the fading keening from the king.

On the other side, Raswyn looked down at the dying ember in his hands. He knew his friend wasn't gone, he had simply split for the last time, creating a new Fire Faeling. This was how the Elemental creatures were reborn. However, every rebirth meant a new personality and only some memories carried forward. The guard felt a tear slip down his cheek as he faced the loss of his friend, his King, and his home. He lowered himself to one knee, allowing the new Fire Faeling to say goodbye to it's former life. The ember went out completely, a small pile of ash left in the guard's hand before the wind swept the ashes off into the dawn morning. Raswyn looked around, seeing the trees, hills, and emptiness around him. There was nothing to be seen, no sign of humans or Fae anywhere around. He took a deep breath and headed into the woods, hearing running water not far away. It was time to find a new home and wait.

THE DIRT ROAD was rough and bumpy, filled with rocks and potholes, causing Sansa to be bounced around in the back seat of the car. After hitting her head against the window for the third time, she opened her mouth, turning towards the front seat, where her parents sat, to complain. She quickly remembered she was still mad, so closed her mouth into a frown, and looked back out the window. The trees and hills rolled by outside the window, the car slowing as it turned the final corner before her grandparents house. Sansa stared at her reflection in the glass, noting the frown above her big, amber colored eyes. Her blonde hair hung straight to her shoulders, with short bangs laying on her forehead, framing her pretty, diamond shaped face. She was six years old, almost seven in two more months, and had two older sisters, Bella, 10, and Katie, 14. Her parents were in the front seat, Mom driving while Dad played with the music, as Bella sat beside her in the backseat.

"We're almost there, Sansa!" Sansa could see her mother's bright red ponytail over the seat in front of her and caught her blue-green eyes looking at her in the rearview mirror.

"It will be fun, you'll see! Lita can't wait to see you, and I think she has plans to take you to a movie, or maybe go swimming. Who knows what else she may be planning!" Sansa looked stonily at her dad, then turned back to look out the window. Her dad sighed from the front seat and, turning to her mom, shrugged in disgruntled acceptance.

Her grandparents lived in the foothills of the Sierra mountains, in Northern California. They owned a house a few miles North of the town Sansa, her sisters, and her parents lived in.

"Sansa, don't be mad." Bella said from the seat beside her. Sansa looked at her sister, still frowning. Bella was going to be flying to Canada for the next two weeks because she was old enough to travel by herself.

Sansa would be going with her too, if only she was 8 instead of 6 and a half. Bella had their father's hair color, a deep brown, but with bright blue eyes framed by glasses, and a heart-shaped face.

"At least you don't have to worry about turbulence or tornados..." Bella was terrified of storms and she was always worried about tornadoes when she was in Canada.

"And at least you get to go on an airplane to another country! And you'll be on the farm, with cute sheep, and dogs, and cats!! Nana spoils you whenever you go." Sansa crossed her arms and turned back to the window, fighting tears.

Sansa was happy to see her grandparents, but it just wasn't fair. Her parents and oldest sister, Katie, were going down to Los Angeles for a State wide Science Fair, and Sansa wanted to go - with either of her sisters! Instead, she was stuck at her grandparents' house, close to home, for two weeks. Katie wasn't with them for the ride to Papo & Lita's. Instead, she was at home, finishing packing for their trip. She was super smart and always trying to teach her sisters about science, chemistry and biology. Katie's hair was black, her eyes blue, and she went by "Sissy" to her little sisters. Although Sansa was

upset about not going to L.A., she was even more upset that Bella was traveling to Canada to see their other grandparents. Sansa was stuck, only a few miles from home, with no kids her age to play with and nothing fun to do!

The car slowed and eventually stopped in front of a bright yellow, two story house nestled in a clearing, surrounded by trees and hills. There was a wooden deck that wrapped around the front entrance and the opposite side, with flowers spilling out of pots set around it. Sansa knew that there was even an old, abandoned gold mine somewhere on the property.

As her parents climbed out of the car and started unloading Sansa's suitcases and backpack, the girls' grandparents stepped out of the front door.

"Sans'!" Papo called excitedly, using his nickname for her, as Lita followed closely behind. Papo's blue eyes were alight with excitement, his hair slightly gray and cut close to his ears. He walked up to Sansa's parents, patting his son on the back as he waited for Sansa to finish climbing out of the car. Sansa straightened, frowning at her parents and grandparents as they all stood together. Bella ran over to them, and Sansa noticed once again, just how much Bella and Lita looked alike. They both had long brown hair, the same heart-shaped face, but where Bella's eyes were a bright blue, Lita had brown eyes like Sansa's dad.

"Still not happy?" her grandmother asked her dad.

"Nope. She doesn't think it's fair that she can't go to L.A. She doesn't realize how not fun it's going to be at the Science Fair. Don't tell Katie, but I wouldn't be going if I didn't have to!" Her dad laughed, but Sansa glared at him as she stomped past to go inside.

"Sansa, do you have hugs for us? You should also say goodbye to Bella before we take her to the airport." Sansa's mom called to her.

She turned around, going back to begrudgingly hug her sister. Bella gave Sansa an extra squeeze and whispered, "Don't stay mad at them- you'll have fun. I know it!"

Sansa stopped and gave her mom and dad a half-hearted hug before running inside, tears starting to run down her cheeks.

A few minutes later, Sansa sat on the couch, blowing her nose and trying to wipe away her tears as her grandparents came in. They sat down on either side of her and leaned in to hug Sansa as they all listened to her parents' car driving back down the dirt road. They were heading back home to pick up Katie before taking Bella to the airport and starting their drive down to L.A. As the tears slowed and Sansa started to feel calmer, Lita offered to make her a treat to help her feel better. Sansa nodded, giving her grandmother a small, sad smile.

After Lita made Sansa an ice cream sundae - complete with chocolate sauce, whipped cream, and sprinkles- Sansa went outside to watch Papo do some yard work. Sometimes, she would help Papo plant or water the flowers, and every once in a while, Lita let her pick a few flowers to keep in a small cup with water. Today, though, she just wanted to watch Papo water the flowers and do some other yard work.

As she watched him get the lawnmower started, Sansa caught sight of a bright flash of color near the trees. She jumped up, crossing the deck to see what had caught her eye. As she searched the trees, trying to see into the shadows, something rushed at her. Sansa jumped back, looked up, and found herself face to face with a tiny hummingbird. She laughed in surprise, giggling at the flashing bird with it's beautiful color as it hovered just in front of her, watching. As suddenly as it had charged at her, it seemed to look over her shoulder, then turned and flew back off into the trees.

"What are you doing over here Sans'?" Papo asked from behind her. Sansa looked over her shoulder, smiling at her grandfather.

"I just saw the most beautiful hummingbird, Papo!" Sansa cried in delight. "She came over just to see me!" She proceeded to tell him all about the bird's colors, the way she seemed to be looking right at her, and how she thought Papo had scared her away. She had already forgotten all about how mad and upset she had been earlier. Papo laughed at her excited chatter, patted her on the back, and headed back to the lawnmower.

Sansa sat back down on the deck, looked towards the forest, and hoped to see her feathery new friend again. Sansa gazed at the world around her, filled with different shades of green and brown. The trees were tall, reaching high to the blue sky above. Although the lawnmower currently drowned out any other sounds, Sansa knew she would hear the rustle of leaves and songs of different birds found in the woods once her Papo was done. After a few minutes, Sansa heard a loud crack from the side of the house, followed by loud exclamations from her grandparents. There was a moment of deafening silence as Papo turned off the lawnmower, before her grandmother ran out the front door, dashed around the deck, and headed towards the back of the house. Sansa curiously followed her to where Papo was standing, glaring at the downstairs bedroom window.

"What on earth happened?" Lita asked Papo.

"Looks like the lawnmower hit a rock and shot it towards the window." Papo answered, running a hand through his hair in frustration.

Sansa looked at the bedroom window, seeing the broken glass scattered around the ground below the window. Lita turned, spotted Sansa, and began walking towards her.

"Let's go inside to get a broom and dustpan so we

can help Papo clean this up." Lita suggested, already shuffling Sansa towards the garage to get the necessary supplies to tidy up the mess.

"What are you going to do with the window? What if a bird flies into the house -or bugs???" Sansa hated bugs, she thought they had too many legs and always *creeped* her out."Papo will figure something out -he'll probably tape it up until we can get someone out here to get it fixed. Don't you worry, we'll make sure no bugs get in." Lita hugged Sansa gently before they headed back outside to sweep up the glass. As they were cleaning, Sansa told her grandmother about the hummingbird she had seen earlier.

"Mom always says that her Nana loved hummingbirds. She told me that if I see one, it's Other-One Nana checking in on me. Do you think that's true?" Sansa looked inquisitively at her grandmother.

"I think those we love, and who love us, always find a way to let us know they are nearby and to check in with us." Lita told Sansa, smiling softly as she swept the shards of glass into the dustpan Sansa held. "I feel my father around sometimes, as if he's just saying a quick hello."

Sansa seemed to ponder that, thinking about how

strange it would be to have dead family visiting you. Even stranger to be the one visiting....

"Do you believe in ghosts, Lita? Or magic?" Lita took a moment before answering her, pausing to think.

"It's hard to understand something we can't see or prove. But I do believe there is more to the world around us than what we can see." Lita carefully stood up with the garbage bag full of broken glass. "Why don't we go inside and get you a snack while I finish cleaning inside."

"Thanks, Lita." Sansa gave her grandmother a quick hug, "I love you. I'm glad I get to spend time with you and Papo. I just wish..." Sansa sniffled, remembering that her parents had left her there.

"Sansa, baby, your parents aren't trying to punish you, or leave you out. The Science Fair isn't a place for a little girl. There are no kids, no toys or games, and no time to visit anywhere fun. They thought it might be better here, with us, than stuck in a hotel room at night and a boring gymnasium during the day. And you know we were very happy to have our little girl with us for a nice visit. Plus, this way I get to go see a movie, and stock the house with sweets!" Lita gave Sansa a one-armed hug, kissing the top of her head. "Now let's go and get you that snack."

Sansa held on for an extra moment, wiping away the tears that had slipped out while Lita was talking. As Sansa stepped away, Lita opened the door and they headed into the house, smiling at each other. Papo was already inside, with his own garbage bag and his phone.

"I called the window shop. They'll have a team out later today to look at the window and give us the bad news of how much it's going to cost us. Stupid rock." Papo frowned.

Sansa giggled "Papo!!! Mom said we're not allowed to say that word!!!"

"Well don't tell her then!" Papo laughed and bent over to hug Sansa tightly, Lita laughing with them.

*****

After some men from the local window repair company came to look at, and measure, the broken window, it was time for dinner.

"Now that we're done with that, what would you like to eat for dinner, Sans'?" Asked her Papo.

"Pizza!" Sansa couldn't help shouting the answer with excitement.

"Why am I not surprised? I suppose you'd like ranch dressing as a dip, too?" Lita laughed.

"Of course, Lita!" Sansa grinned at her grandmother.

After picking up and enjoying pizza from a local restaurant in town, Sansa and her grandparents sat down to watch a movie. Lita made some popcorn for everyone to share while Sansa snuggled into a blanket with her favorite stuffy, Darla the magical dragon. An hour into the movie, Lita's phone started to ring. Sansa jumped up in excitement.

"Is that Bella? Or Mom and Dad?" Sansa leaned over her grandmother's shoulder, trying to see who was calling. Before she could make out a name on the display, Lita answered.

"Hi, Bella.....Yes, your sister is right here." Lita handed the phone to Sansa, who snuggled back into the couch so she could comfortably listen to her sister tell her about her trip. A little while later, Sansa hung up the phone, stifling a yawn.

"Was Bella's trip ok?" Lita asked.

"Yes. She said the flight was good and she's at Nana and Poppa's farm now. She's getting ready for bed, but wants to see all the farm animals in the morning. I wish I could see the animals, too." Sansa looked sad again, but no tears came this time.

"You will both have great adventures over the next couple of weeks. And when you and your sisters are all back together, you can share everything fun you've each done. But for now, it is bedtime for you." Lita called for Papo as she folded Sansa's blanket, then led her upstairs to the guest room, Papo following behind them.

As they reached the top of the stairs, Sansa looked around. On the right hand side was an open office with a desk, chair, a couple of couches, and an old armoire. Ahead of her, in between the two rooms, was a small bathroom, and to the left was the guest room where she would be sleeping. Upstairs was painted a soft cream, highlighted with shades of brown and gold. Sansa noticed her suitcases were stacked in a corner, and the comforter was pulled down - ready for her to crawl in to the double bed.

"You know where everything is, and we'll be downstairs if you need us. Your parents even left you some cool glow sticks!! Do you need anything else?" Lita asked her as she tucked Sansa into bed.

"No thanks, Lita. Goodnight." Sansa yawned and

gave her grandparents a sleepy smile.

Papo leaned over to give Sansa a hug and kiss, wished her a goodnight, and stepped aside so Lita could do the same. They both gave Sansa one more smile before leaving the room, heading downstairs.

After she heard her grandparents reach the bottom of the stairs, Sansa slid out from under the blankets, kneeled on the bed, and opened the closed blinds above her bed to look out at the moon. It was hanging brightly in the night sky, and as she kneeled there, she saw the first star appear in the sky."Star light, star bright, first star I see tonight...I wish I may, I wish I might, have my wish I wish tonight.... I wish to have an amazing adventure, filled with magic and fun." Sansa yawned again, closed the blinds, and crawled back into bed. Once she was comfortable, she closed her eyes and fell into a deep sleep. That night she dreamt of the bright hummingbird she had seen and a large, green forest, alive with magical creatures.

2

"**W**HERE DID YOU go?" Sansa called softly into the dark forest around her. She looked around carefully, searching for the bright flash of the little bird's wings. The shadows were long despite the moon shining brightly above.

"Aha!!" Sansa called out as she saw her new friend fly back towards her. "Am I running too slow?" The hummingbird kept flying ahead and circling back, it's little wings moving quicker than Sansa's little legs.

The hummingbird flew around her head in a circle before darting off to the side and hovering near a few small pine trees. The moonlight shimmered softly off the bird's wings, giving it a magical glow.

"You want me to go that way? Ok, I'm coming!" Sansa laughed as she started running towards the hummingbird once more.

She pushed between the smaller trees eagerly, catching her leggings on the prickly berry bushes hidden behind them. Sansa felt a tug on her left leg, followed by the sharp pain of something scratching her. Sansa looked down to see where the thorns of the berry bushes had torn through her pants and left an angry red line on her calf. As tears started to well up, the hummingbird flew over and down to where her leg was starting to bleed. The bird seemed to examine the leg before flying back up to Sansa's face, hovering there as though waiting to see what the little girl would do. So Sansa did the only thing she could: she took a deep breath, wiped her sleeve over her eyes, and pushed through the bushes. The hummingbird did a little dance in the air before flying ahead of the little girl.

Sansa tried to keep up with the quick bird while trying not to get any more scratches from the brambles and branches around her. She noticed spears of bright light coming from ahead of her, but she wasn't scared of the light or it's source. She knew her feathery friend had flown ahead and she needed to find out where it was taking her. Sansa pushed through more bushes, thankful that there seemed to be no more thorns or brambles ahead. She stumbled over a large root and a fallen tangle of branches, but managed not to fall to her knees as she burst into the clearing.

Sansa straightened, looking around at the trees and hills that spread out below her. She turned and saw that she had come through the forest and was standing at the top of a hill. The moon was shining over the hillside, it's bright light making the trees glisten around her. The sounds of owls, frogs, and other nocturnal creatures, created a soft hum in the otherwise silent night. Now that Sansa was in the clearing, she could see that the moon was not the source of the bright light she had seen through the trees. On the other side of the clearing stood a giant, twisted tree. The roots were visible above ground, the limbs seeming to curve and weave into intricate designs, covered by leaves of every color, and in the middle of the wide trunk there was what appeared to be a doorway with light seeping through. As Sansa watched the tree, the light became brighter, and it seemed as if the door was opening. Sansa found herself stepping forward, towards the bright light pouring from the door, her hand *outstretched. She squinted as she stepped into the light, momentarily blinded. Her heart raced, the scratches on her legs were forgotten as she felt herself pass through the portal....*

Sansa sat up suddenly, her heart racing even as she noticed the sun spilling across her bed. She looked around at the spare bedroom of her grandparent's house, trying to reorient herself. Her suitcases still stood in the corner, and Darla was face down on the floor.

"It was...a dream?" Sansa whispered to herself, reaching down to pick up and squeeze the little dragon.

She sat up and swung her legs over the side of the bed, her leg rubbing against the blanket. As it did, a sharp pain rippled up from her calf. Sansa carefully pulled the blanket back, tugged her pajama leg up, and gasped when she saw a long scratch with streaks of dried blood. Sansa quickly stood, running to the bathroom to wipe off her leg. The scratch was tender and sore, but Sansa didn't think it needed a band-aid.

She didn't know what she would tell Papo and Lita about the scratch on her leg, so she decided the best choice was to avoid talking about it. As she picked out long pants that would cover the scratch, Sansa was thankful that at least she wouldn't have to worry that

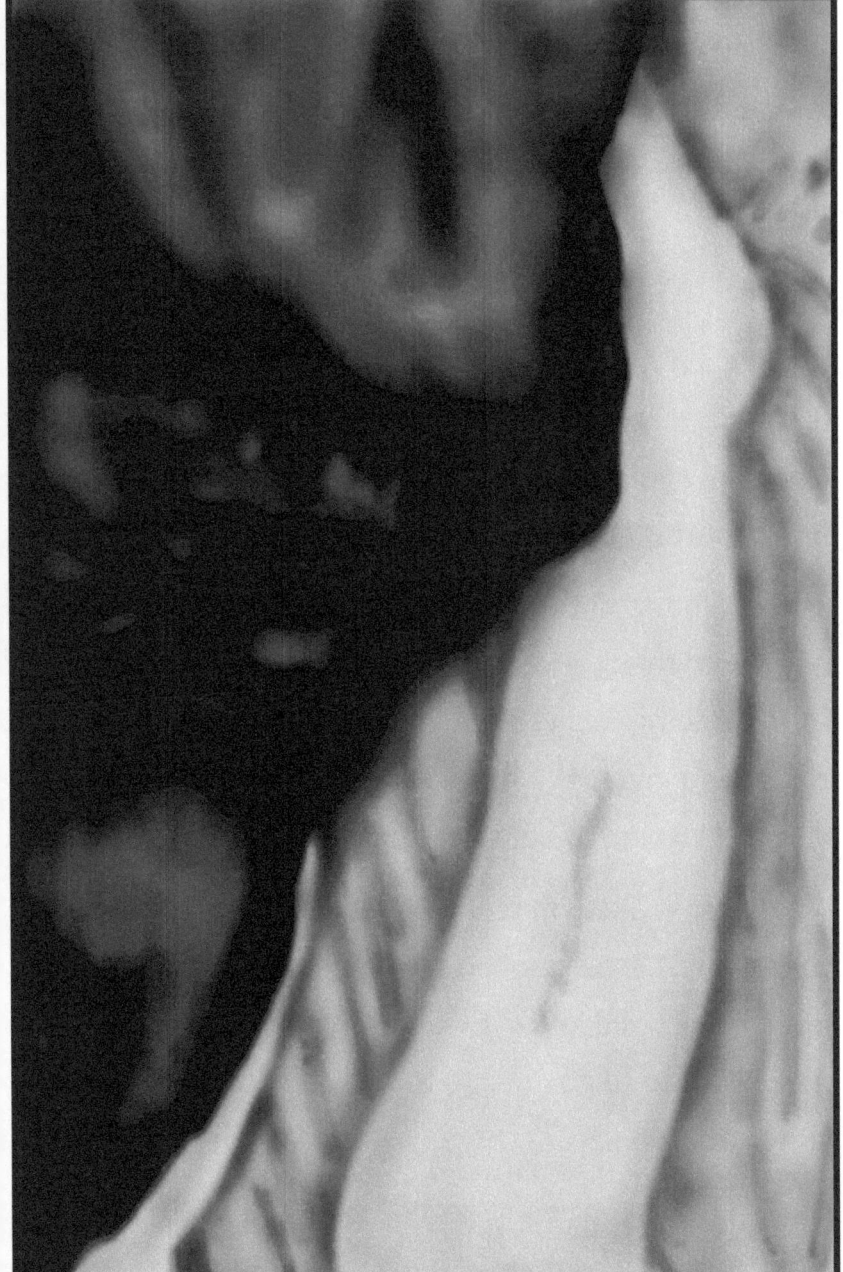

Papo and Lita might think she did something wrong - like sneaking out or something. After getting dressed, Sansa headed down the stairs, where she could hear her Papo humming in the kitchen, and the scent of bacon wafting in the air.

"Hey there, Sans'! I thought I would make you breakfast this morning!" Papo came over to Sansa, bending over to give her a hug and a kiss on the top of her head. He then leaned into her ear and whispered, "You know your parents and sisters aren't getting a breakfast this good today," causing Sansa to giggle.

"What's all that whispering about in here?" Lita asked with mock severity as she walked into the kitchen. After stopping to give Papo a quick kiss, she moved over to Sansa to give her a hug and kiss too. "What's with the pants? It's going to be warm today."

"Yeah, Lita. I'm feeling a little cold so I decided to wear pants." Sansa looked down, embarrassed at telling her Lita a lie. She knew it was wrong, but she really, really wanted to go outside today. Lita put her hand to Sansa's forehead.

"I hope you're not getting sick. You'll tell Lita if you don't feel well, right?"

Sansa looked up at her Lita, "I feel fine Lita, I promise! I'm just a little cold and tired. Papo's yummy breakfast will make me feel warm and wake me up!"

She smiled first at her Lita, then at her Papo, who was standing at the stove again. Lita gave her another quick squeeze before gently pushing Sansa towards the dining room.

"Go set the table, then, little girl! I'm starving!"

After setting the table, Sansa looked at her Lita guiltily, the lie still weighing on her. She wanted to tell the truth. She never lied to Lita, or Papo, because they understood her. They really listened to her; no matter what happened, they didn't just pat her on the head and say something about only being 6. But how could they understand this when she didn't even know what happened? Sansa rubbed at her leg, just above the scratch, trying to think about how she might have scratched herself. Did she do it while she was sleeping? Did it happen yesterday and she just didn't remember? There was a lot of glass.... Or was it magic?

Sansa decided that as soon as she knew what happened, she would tell Papo and Lita. Until then, she would work on figuring it out so she could tell them the whole truth.

Once breakfast was done and the dishwasher was loaded, Sansa was in a hurry to get outside.

"Lita, can I go outside for a bit this morning?"

"Of course! But don't go too far. Papo and I are waiting for the installers from the window place to come replace the glass this morning, so we can't play with you right now."

"Ok, Lita." Sansa smiled at her grandmother before putting her shoes on. As she bent over, her leggings pulled up a little, showing a bit of the scratch on her leg. Sansa quickly laced up her shoes, pulled her leggings back down, and raced outside.

"Sansa, wait!" Lita called after her.

Sansa stopped, worried that her grandmother had noticed the scratch when she had bent over. She turned around slowly, looking down at her feet, waiting for Lita to ask to look at her leg. She knew she would tell the truth if Lita asked.

"Take this bottle of water with you. It's going to be another hot day." Lita handed Sansa a cold bottle of water from the fridge before giving her a quick hug. "Now remember- not too far!"

Sansa took the bottle of water from her

grandmother gratefully, and smiled at her before turning to run down the steps. As she heard the front door close behind her, Sansa headed towards the trees to the side of the house. She glanced back once, guiltily, before carefully stepping into the woods.

The woods were shadowed, with the shade falling over Sansa in cool silence. She could hear the birds in the trees and the rustle of leaves around her. She thought she heard branches crackling as though being stepped on, but the sound was gone a moment later. She took a deep breath, tucked the bottle of water into her sweater pocket, and headed deeper into the forest. Sansa tried to remember her dream from the night before. Were these the trees in her dream? She closed her eyes, trying to picture what the forest looked like, but all she could recall was that it had been darker, with shadows stretched all around. So Sansa opened her eyes and started walking through the woods, no set destination in mind.

Sansa tried to keep track of time, stopping and listening for her Papo and Lita. At one point, she thought she heard a truck driving up the road, the mumble of a few voices talking all at once, then a door closing. The workers must be at the house now, which meant that

Sansa had a bit of time before Lita or Papo would be looking for her. As she continued to explore, looking for a break in the trees or the weird tree from her dream, Sansa thought she heard the same sound she'd heard earlier. It almost sounded like someone was walking in the woods with her. She kept hearing the crackle of breaking branches, but whenever she stopped to listen, the sound would stop too. It didn't help that, with all the trees and bushes around, the sound seemed to be coming from different directions around her.

Soon, Sansa realized that not only had she lost track of time, but she had also become disoriented. She stopped in her tracks, looking around frantically for something that looked familiar. She listened intently for the sound of workers, her grandparents, or even a truck driving. Tears started to well up in her eyes as Sansa began to feel afraid, her heart racing in her chest. As she turned in circles, panic rising, she spotted something red to the right of her, half hidden in the bushes. The color and shape teased at a memory, but she couldn't remember what it reminded her of.

Sansa took a deep breath, wiped her tears with her sleeve, and headed towards the bushes.

As she reached them, she realized that what she had spotted was a deflated red ball. Sansa crouched down, looking at it curiously when another bright flash of color caught her eye.

A little ways ahead, there was something blue hidden in the brush, just like the red ball. She started walking towards the blue, then spotted another deflated ball, just up ahead, but black and white this time. It was as if someone was laying a trail for Sansa using old, flat balls. Sansa remembered how many balls, all different colors, had been lost in the trees around her Grandparents' house. She kept following the swatches of color, ball after ball, until she could see the yellow house through the trees. As she ran out of the trees, her heart racing, Sansa's grandparents stepped out of the house.

"Sansa! We were just coming out to look for you. The installers are done with the window, and it's almost lunch time. Did you have fun playing outside?"

Sansa ran up the stairs, throwing herself into her Papo's arms. She looked over her shoulder, unsure of what had happened in the trees- she still had so many questions.... Why were her lost balls in the trees? Was someone following her? And who, or what, had helped her find her way out of the woods?

3

THE NEXT MORNING, Sansa lay in bed, thinking about the previous day. Getting lost in the woods had been scary, but the deflated balls that led her out of the trees made her want to go back. She could say it was out of curiosity, but it was more than that. There was something going on in the forest and she wanted - needed - to find out what it was.

After she had run into Papo's arms, her grandparents kept her close for the rest of the day. They had lunch, then went to see a movie before running to the grocery store. Lita put on a TV show for Sansa in the living room while Lita and Papo unloaded groceries then started dinner. After dinner, Sansa's parents called so she could talk to them and, very briefly, Katie before getting ready for bed. Thankfully, there were no more strange dreams and no mysterious scratches.

As she lay in bed the next morning, remembering, Sansa started to hear movement downstairs. She decided to get out of bed and go down for breakfast. After washing up and making her bed, Sansa headed downstairs.

"Good morning, Papo & Lita!" Sansa called when she got to the bottom of the stairs.

"Good morning, sweetie." Lita came over to hug her.

"Where's Papo?" Sansa asked.

"He ran to the hardware store to pick up some things for outside. He's thinking about building you girls a treehouse!"

"That would be awesome!" Sansa said excitedly. "Bella and I could play hide and seek or pirates or princesses in the castle! Where would he build it? How big would it be? How long will it take to build?!" Sansa couldn't help peppering her grandmother with questions.

"You'll have to ask your Papo, but it probably won't be finished until after your parents and sisters come home." Lita laughed. "Awww..." Sansa was momentarily disappointed, but the fact that they might get a cool treehouse this summer was still exciting.

"What do you want to do this morning, Lita?" Sansa wasn't sure what she wanted to do, but maybe Lita had some good ideas.

"Oh, I'm sorry, honey, when Papo gets back, we have to do some work upstairs, in the office. Maybe after lunch we can do something? For now, I can make you breakfast.

"Oh, okay. Breakfast sounds good." Sansa was feeling disappointed again, as she followed Lita into the kitchen.

After eating a bowl of her favorite cereal that Lita had bought especially for her visit, Sansa went to put on her shoes. She grabbed a bottle of water and a sweater, then headed out the door just in time to see Papo's truck driving up the road to the house. Sansa smiled and waved as he slowly pulled up, the back of his red truck full of lumber.

"Sansa!" Papo got out of the truck and walked over to hug her. "Do you see what's in the back of the truck? I'm going to build a cool treehouse for your Lita...."

Sansa started laughing. "Lita doesn't need a treehouse!"

"Uh-oh…. Who am I going to build a treehouse for, then? Are you sure she wouldn't like to live in a treehouse?"

Sansa laughed and nodded. She knew Papo loved to tease her and her sisters.

"Am I going to be able to help you build it?" Sansa asked, "That would be super cool!!"

"I'm sure I can find some work for you. Hopefully you build better than your dad - Did I ever tell you about that time he and I built the wall upstairs? Let me tell you, it's a good thing he's not a construction worker…." Papo put his arm around Sansa and led her inside, regaling her with the story of the time he worked with her dad to build the wall separating the bedroom and the office. Sansa listened intently, laughing as she pictured her dad messing up while measuring the wood, or even being unable to hammer in a nail properly. Papo may have exaggerated just a little bit, but the story made Sansa forget about her disappointments that morning.

After Papo finished his story, it was time for him and Lita to go upstairs to do some work. Sansa wasn't sure what she was going to do, but decided to sit outside for a little bit. Since she still had her sweater and water, she ran out the door, heading to the deck to sit and think about what she wanted to do. She could watch T.V, or play with her toys, or read her comics, or... go explore the trees. As Sansa sat on the deck, there was a loud crack in the woods, off to the left of her.

"Hello?" Sansa called out tentatively. "Is anyone there?"

She thought she saw a flash of color partially hidden by the trees and stood, looking over her shoulder at the door. Should she get her grandparents or go investigate on her own? If she did investigate, what could she do to make sure she didn't get lost? Sansa looked around, wondering if there was anything she could use to mark her path. A breeze blew past her, causing a colored strip of tape to wave in the corner of her eye. Papo had tied the tape to the lumber in the back of the truck. Walking over to the truck, Sansa saw that he had a roll of the orange tape in the back. She picked it up and tucked it into her pocket. The tape would be put to good use if she could just tear pieces off and tie them to branches. That way she could find her way back if she was lost again. Heart racing, Sansa headed into the woods, looking for a sign of the fluttering she had seen from the deck.

As she carefully started walking through the bushes, Sansa thought she heard more cracks ahead of her. Once again, it sounded as though someone was walking through the bushes, crunching leaves and branches beneath their feet. Sansa stopped, taking a deep breath. She was hesitant to follow whoever was ahead of her, remembering how her parents told her to be wary of strangers. As she was getting ready to turn around and go back to the house, Sansa felt a small puff of air on her cheek. She turned and saw the beautiful hummingbird only a few inches away.

"Oh! Hello again! I was just going to go back to the house...." The bird moved side to side, tilting it's head while staring at Sansa. Then, just like in her dream, it turned and started flying towards the noise Sansa had heard earlier. It stopped, turned back to look at her, and waited. Sansa glanced over her shoulder, then looked back to the hummingbird for a minute before making her decision. She had to find out what was going on. The hummingbird, the dreams, the flat balls when she was lost, the strange sounds- there was something going on and she had to know what it was. She had wished for magic and adventure, so she was going to be brave and go looking for it!

As Sansa stepped forward, the hummingbird flew ahead. Sansa stopped briefly to tie a piece of orange tape to the closest tree, then followed the bird, stopping every once in a while to tie another piece of tape. Sansa went deeper into the trees than she had before, glancing back every few minutes just to make sure she could follow the tape home. She carefully stepped through berry bushes, cautiously making sure not to scratch herself, while watching for the hummingbird flitting ahead of her. She listened for noises in the woods around her, and soon, Sansa began to hear something that sounded like running water up ahead.

Sansa noticed that the ground was getting rougher, the bushes becoming sparser before eventually giving way to stones and rocks. The trees seemed to be getting further apart, and Sansa could see light shining through the trees ahead of her. The hummingbird flew through the branches and leaves and into the light, from where Sansa could clearly hear water rushing over rocks. A few steps later, Sansa was pushing some of the low hanging branches aside, temporarily blinded by the bright sun shining into her eyes. She covered her eyes, looking around in surprise. She didn't remember Papo or Lita saying anything about a stream near their house. It was only about 6 feet wide and looked to be about 3 or 4 feet deep, but the water was moving fast over large rocks and boulders. Across the creek, there were more trees lining the edge. Sansa quickly tied some orange tape to a branch behind her before moving closer to the water. It was so clear that she thought she saw fish darting between the rocks, moving downstream with the water.

Sansa bent down to feel the water, immediately surprised at how cold it was. As she was bent over, there was a large cracking sound behind her. Startled, Sansa stood up quickly, causing her foot to start slipping on the slick rocks. She tried to catch her balance, but found herself stumbling closer to the water instead. Sansa cried out, twisting to catch herself and failing, falling onto the rocks. She felt her foot slide into the cold liquid and gasped as the icy cold covered her leg up to her knee. The water was deeper than it looked and Sansa's heart was racing as she continued to fall. Suddenly she felt a jerk on her sweater, and she realized she was being pulled out of the creek, off the rocks, and about 3 feet into the air. Sansa had closed her eyes while falling, but now they popped wide open as she screamed in surprise. She tried looking behind her, but since she was hanging in the air, all she could do was kick her legs and swing wildly about.

A couple of moments later, she was gently placed back on solid ground, a few feet from the edge of the stream. Sansa's legs were shaking, so it took a moment for her to get her balance. As soon as she felt stable enough, she tentatively turned to see who had rescued her from the water. At first, all she saw was what looked like a tree trunk, so she looked up....and up....and up...and shrieked in shock. Her 7-foot tall rescuer jumped and cried out in surprise in response to Sansa's reaction.

Sansa's eyes widened as she looked at the large brown and green creature standing before her. Not only was the creature tall, but he looked like he was made up of the forest around him. His body was as broad as a tree trunk, and his skin was green with what appeared to be bark across his chest and shoulders. There also seemed to be what looked like moss spreading in patches across his chest, arms, and what little Sansa could see of his back. His face was craggy, with a rocky brow; deep-set, bright green eyes; high and sharp cheekbones; two large fangs jutting up from behind his

large, bottom lip; and a large nose.

"Th-th-thank y-you...." Sansa whispered weakly, not sure if she was shaking with cold or with fear. The creature blinked down at her.

"I'm Sansa...." Sansa managed to not stutter this time, and she was glad her voice was stronger and sounded normal. "What's your name?""Sannnnnssssssaaa.....?" The creature's voice sounded rusty and unused as he slowly pronounced her name.

"I....Tanrawdtatoeraswyn."

"Ummmm, Tanra....tatos.....win...." Sansa struggled to repeat his name, so asked instead, "Can I call you Tato?"

Tato nodded, blinking slowly down at her. They stood like that for a few minutes, staring in awe at each other until Sansa remembered her wet foot and looked down, shaking her leg to try and get the excess water off. Tato looked down at her leg, too.

"Papo and Lita are never going to let me outside again after this!!" Sansa sighed. She looked back up at Tato, accidentally startling him. He had been bending down closer to try and get a better look at her leg. He stood back up quickly, eyes going wide once again. Sansa giggled softly.

"Do you live here - in the forest?" She asked gently. Tato nodded and looked off to the left of them, upstream of the creek. Sansa could see the trees continued on either side of the creek, heading up the hill.

"Did you help me the other day? When I was lost?" Tato nodded again. "Thanks.... Were those my lost balls you used? I thought those were gone forever."

"I...have them.... I keep...presents." Tato said

slowly.

"Do you live here alone?" Sansa gently touched Tato's hand, worried that he was lonely, living out in the woods.

Tato shook his head. "I have friends..." Tato looked around them, searching in the sky above them. His face lit up after he spotted what he was looking for. The hummingbird Sansa had been following flew down and landed on Tato's shoulder. He grinned at the tiny bird perched on him before looking back at Sansa and pointing at the bird. "Friend." He then pointed at Sansa. "Are you friend too?"

Sansa grinned back at the big troll, nodded, and stuck out her hand. "Friend."

4

THAT NIGHT, SANSA couldn't go to sleep. She was replaying the events of the day over and over again in her mind. It was so hard to believe that she had met such an unusual creature like Tato! After he had taken her hand in his, he had just held it, as if he had not had human contact in so long he had forgotten. His language had improved as they spoke more, and the hummingbird followed the pair as they made their way to Tato's home. The three new friends followed the creek upstream, approaching a rocky outcropping covered in moss, climbing vines, and bushes. Sansa couldn't see the doorway until they were upon it. The greenery seemed to shimmer before her, revealing a path through the foliage.

As soon as she saw the entrance, Sansa realized Tato's home must be the old mine entrance!

As they entered the cave, she began looking around. To the right of the entrance was a fire pit, a low flame flickering within, with a few large boulders nearby and several broken lawn chairs. There appeared to be a sleeping area towards the back of the cave, made up of furs, leaves, and ragged pieces of fabric. Towards the front of the mine entrance, there was a little pool of water, seeming to fill from a natural, bubbling spring in the ground. The cave was cozy and warm, but large enough for Tato to stand straight up and still have room to stretch his arms above his head.

While the hummingbird flew over to a nest on a rock jutting out in the corner, Tato walked towards the fire and Sansa placed her wet socks and shoes where they could dry from the heat before sitting on one of the boulders.

She wasn't sure how strong the chairs were and didn't want to chance breaking one. Tato leaned towards the fire, whispering softly, although Sansa could not understand a word of what he was saying. Then, to Sansa's surprise, a small creature made of flickering tongues of orange and yellow, stepped out of the fire and walked towards Tato. As the tiny fire-being neared Tato, he started speaking in another language, clearly upset with the large troll. Tato looked mildly embarrassed as he hung his head. When the creature was done, Tato gestured to Sansa and responded in the same tongue. After the two spent some time going back and forth, Sansa shook her head, completely confused. Finally, Tato cleared his throat and frowned down at the small flame. The creature flared blue and red for a moment before turning and glaring at Sansa.

"This is Lasair. Friend." Tato looked down at Lasair, pointing his head towards Sansa and frowning. Lasair finally responded, nodding stiffly to her before sitting on a small rock at the base of one of the beat up looking chairs. After glancing back and forth between Sansa and Lasair, Tato seemed to decide it was safe to leave them alone for a few minutes.

Tato walked to an area where shelves were made from different sized tree trunks and large branches. At one end, a pile of worn and warped books were stacked, while at the other end, it appeared that there were old tin bowls and cups - the kind Sansa had learned were used by miners or campers, and what appeared to be thick bark slabs made into plates. Tato put some berries and nuts in one of the bowls and brought it over to Sansa. He then took one of the cups to the spring and filled it with clear, cold water for her to drink. They sat next to the fire silently, both seeming at a loss for words. After a few minutes, Sansa cleared her throat softly.

"Tato...? Why do you live here?" Sansa asked tentatively.

"I watch the door. Protect it." Tato stuttered less now, finding it easier to remember English, as well as speaking to someone other than Lasair and his hummingbird friend.

"Door? You mean the entrance to the mine?" Sansa was confused. She didn't see any doors anywhere. She wondered if he chose the wrong word and tried to think of what he could have meant.

Tato shook his head sadly before answering. "No, the door in tree. It is the door to home."

Sansa was only getting more confused. She didn't know how to tell Tato that trees didn't have doors - especially a door to anyone's home.

"Where is home?" Sansa asked instead.

"Other side of door. It is a magic land, filled with Fairies. I miss it." Lasair looked up at Tato in surprise. Tato glanced sadly at Lasair before looking over to Sansa, tears in his eyes. Sansa climbed off the rock and walked over to him cautiously, aware of her bare feet and the tiny flame near Tato's chair. She imagined how lonely he must feel with just a bird and a fire creature for friends, living almost alone in the mine, so far away from his home.

"Why do you stay then? If there's a door, why can't you go home? Do you have family there? They must miss you...."

"Tato and Lasair protect door. We guard and wait." Tato sighed sadly as tears started to fall, continuing, "My family is gone. Bad fairies and humans took them, and my friends."

"Oh Tato.... I'm so sorry." Sansa tried to hug Tato,

although he was too big for her to wrap her arms all the way around him. He sat still for a minute, seemingly unsure of what to do with the hug. Then he slowly wrapped his arms around Sansa and hugged her back as he cried. After a few minutes, the tears slowed and Tato took a deep breath. He smiled at Sansa, amazed at the little person comforting him. The fact that she could see him and his magical home was surprising, but that she was so kind and generous was a gift.

After visiting a little longer, Sansa started to worry about her grandparents. She put on her dried socks and shoes, then got ready for Tato to lead her home. Before stepping out of the cave, Sansa turned to Lasair.

"It was nice meeting you, Lasair." She smiled gently at the small flame fae. He grudgingly nodded back before turning back to watch the fire.

As they walked through the woods, Sansa told Tato about her sisters, parents, and grandparents. Too soon, they were approaching the edge of the forest, close enough that Sansa could see the house through the trees. They both stopped and she turned and hugged Tato tightly.

"I'll come back tomorrow, I promise!" Sansa smiled up at her new friend. She waited until Tato smiled back before turning to run to the house.

After finding Papo and Lita still at work upstairs, Sansa

grabbed some crackers and cheese out of the fridge, then sat down to eat her lunch. The rest of the afternoon flew by, and Sansa couldn't wait to go to bed so she could see Tato again the next day. She rushed through dinner, watched TV with her Lita, talked to Bella, then headed straight up to bed, excited for the next day.

What Sansa didn't realize was that her grandparents had plans for her in the morning. She wasn't known to be patient, and the fact that she couldn't see Tato the next morning irritated her.

When Lita asked her to get dressed to go out, Sansa found herself whining; then, when Papo and Lita decided to go out for lunch, instead of enjoying herself, Sansa had to fight back tears. Papo and Lita could tell something was bothering her, but they couldn't understand what might have upset her other than possibly missing her parents and sisters. There was no way they could have known that it was simply because she wanted to go out to play in the forest with her new friend!

As they were eating, Lita tried talking to Sansa about activities they could do together that afternoon. Papo and Lita felt bad for how little time they had been able to spend with her since she arrived, so they really wanted to have a fun day together. "So, have you decided what we should do this afternoon, Sans?" This was the third time Papo had tried to get a response to their question. Sansa was still angry, so after Papo's innocent question, she found herself yelling at them.

"I just want to play outside by myself!! I don't want to go to the playground or the park; I don't want to play ball or do gardening with Papo! Why won't you just let me go outside?" Tears were streaming down Sansa's red cheeks. Her anger, frustration, and restlessness boiled up and out of her in a streaming mix of whining, crying, and yelling. Her grandparents sat back, shocked at the sudden behavior. After a few moments, Papo stood up, looked at Sansa, and sternly told her they were going home.

"When we get home, you will go to your room. You do not talk to your Lita and I that way young lady!" Papo continued in the car.

"Fine!" Sansa yelled before looking sullenly out the window. As soon as they parked at the house, she stomped up the stairs. "I don't want to do anything fun with you anyway."

As soon as she said it, Sansa regretted it, but she was so angry that she just couldn't seem to stop. Although she wanted to slam the door, she knew that it would only make the situation worse. Sansa threw herself onto the bed, crying into her pillow and wishing that her parents and sisters were there.

Eventually, Sansa's sobs turned to hiccups, her cheeks still hot, and her eyes feeling gritty. She found some tissue, blew her nose, and went into the upstairs bathroom to wash her face. After she came out of the bathroom, she stood quietly at the top of the stairs and listened. She could hear the TV in her grandparents' bedroom, but no sounds otherwise. Sansa really wanted to see Tato, but she knew her grandparents would not let her go outside after her outburst. She could feel tears welling up in the corners of her eyes again, so she took a deep breath and started to tiptoe down the stairs, peeking around the corner to see if there was any sign of her Lita or Papo. She would just sneak into the trees for a few minutes, Sansa told herself - just long enough to tell Tato that she couldn't play with him today. She would be back before they knew she was gone....

Sansa quietly got her shoes on, opening the door as silently as possible. She peered onto the deck and, not seeing anyone, stepped outside and slowly closed the door behind her. She knew she should wait to talk to her grandparents and say sorry for yelling. They might even let her play outside if she did, but she couldn't take that chance - she didn't want to wait! Meeting Tato was the coolest, most exciting thing ever, and she couldn't let her grandparents stop her. Sansa ran over to the trees and was about to step into them when she heard an angry voice behind her....

"Where do you think you're going?" Sansa slowly turned around and looked into the angry face of her Lita. She had forgotten to look around the corner of the deck to see if they were sitting outside....

"I....um...was going to...." Sansa stuttered and trailed off, uncertain of what to say. She didn't think her Lita would believe her about Tato, and even if she did, Papo and Lita might think he was scary or dangerous. He certainly had looked that way until she had seen his eyes - they were full of innocence and kindness.

"You cannot talk to us the way you did at lunch and then sneak out of the house! You are grounded for the rest of the day. Maybe tomorrow, too young lady! Go back inside right now." Lita frowned at Sansa, crossing her arms as she waited for the little girl to listen.

Sansa started crying again. "But Lita - that's not fair!" When Lita continued to frown at her, Sansa turned and ran inside, immediately heading back upstairs to her bed. It was the worst day ever!

After about an hour, as Sansa was laying on her bed, eyes dry again, she heard footsteps on the stairs, followed by a soft knock on her door.

"Can we come in?" Papo asked politely.

Sansa sniffled and sat up. "Okay...."

Papo and Lita came over to her bed, sitting down next to her.

"Do you want to talk about what happened?" Lita asked Sansa. She opened her mouth to say no, instead starting to cry all over again, knowing she had been wrong.

"I'm so sorry... I didn't mean it!" Sansa hiccupped, the sudden, heavy breath breaking up her words. "I just wanted to play outside and I didn't want to wait." She hiccupped again before continuing, "I love you and I'm sorry I yelled and said mean things." Sansa threw herself into her Papo's arms, sobbing into his shoulder. Papo hugged her and Lita started rubbing her back.

"Thank you, sweetheart. We understand that you wanted to play outside, but we wanted to spend time with you too because we've been so busy the past few days! Do you think there were better ways to tell us what you wanted?" Lita asked. Sansa nodded.

"I should have told you nicely that I wanted to play outside…. And I shouldn't have gotten mad that you wanted to do something fun." Sansa wiped her eyes as her Lita passed her a tissue. After blowing her nose and sniffling a few more times, Sansa looked at her grandparents in embarrassment. "I'm so sorry."

"We accept your apology, but there will still be a punishment for yelling and trying to sneak out. You are grounded to the house for the rest of the day, but if you behave and listen, you can go outside tomorrow to play. AND maybe we'll watch a movie tonight." Papo tried frowning at Sansa, but after a moment, he smiled sympathetically and gave her a big hug. Lita leaned in to hug her too, wrapping her arms around Papo and Sansa

"Do you feel like coming downstairs for a bit? We could have a snack, maybe play a game of cards." Lita asked after a few moments.

Sansa nodded again, then followed her grandparents downstairs. The rest of the day passed slowly, spent inside with her grandparents instead of out with Tato like she had wanted. Sansa knew she needed to be more patient, that she needed to wait sometimes instead of rushing into whatever she wanted to do. She promised herself that she would try to be more patient in the future. Hopefully, Tato wouldn't think she had abandoned him, and as soon as she was allowed, she would go say sorry to him, too.

5

THE NEXT MORNING, Sansa woke up early, excited to see Tato. She had been patient and listened all evening and so before bed, her grandparents had said she could play outside in the morning! Sansa was already planning what she wanted to do and what she was going to take for her friend to apologize for not showing up the day before. Sansa thought of his home in the mine and wanted to bring him some things to make it more fun and comfortable. She looked through a shelf of Lita's old towels and blankets in the upstairs closet, finding some old clothes of Papo's, too. Once she had everything together, Sansa folded the items and placed them in a plastic bag before heading down the stairs.

She stopped about halfway down, turned as something occurred to her, and quickly ran back into her room to look at her stuffed animals. Her favorite was sitting in front of the  others - the bright green and pink dragon named Darla. Sansa thought Tato would like her, so she grabbed Darla and threw her into the bag. She was going to miss her, but the thought of Tato having Darla made Sansa smile. She started down the stairs once more, not sure what she was going to tell her grandparents if they asked about her bag.

"Good morning, Sans'!" Papo called to her as she stepped off the bottom step. "Looks like you have a few blankets in there - you thinking about having a picnic in the woods?"

Sansa smiled at her Papo. She hadn't thought of that! "Yup! Can I take some snacks for my picnic?" This was great - she was going to have a picnic with Tato!

"Well, we have some cherries, strawberries, and blueberries in the fridge. And some of those gummies you love in the pantry. Of course, you also need some cookies and juice. Let me help you get everything together. A picnic sounds like a lot of fun!" Papo grabbed his small cooler from the laundry room and started to fill it with a couple of juice boxes, some fruit Sansa had put into a sandwich bag, a pack of fruit gummies, and a few cookies that Papo placed into another sandwich bag.

"Did I hear that someone's having a picnic?" Lita asked as she walked into the kitchen. She spotted Sansa's dragon in her bag, along with the blankets and towels. "Is Darla going to join you? I know you want to play by yourself today, but maybe we could have a picnic with the three of us in a few days?"

"That sounds awesome, Lita!" Sansa beamed at her grandparents as she put on her shoes, took the cooler from her Papo, and picked up the plastic bag again.

"I know there aren't any wild animals or anything in the woods, but please remember to stay close and be safe!" Papo gave Sansa a quick hug and a kiss on her head.

Lita did the same, giving Sansa an extra squeeze as she softly told her, "I'm glad to see you in a better mood today. Go have fun."

Sansa grinned over her shoulder at her grandparents as she rushed out the door, then faced ahead to race down the steps and into the trees. As soon as Sansa stepped into the woods, the cool shadows surrounded her, providing some relief from the early morning warmth. She continued to grin as she followed the orange tape still tied to branches that led to the stream.

She kept looking around, watching for Tato or the hummingbird. She was surprised that she didn't see him before reaching the creek. She watched her step near the rushing water, remembering how cold and deep it was and how slick the rocks had been. She headed upstream and started calling Tato's name.

"Tato! Tato?" Sansa couldn't see the mine entrance, but she remembered how well hidden it was until you walked right up to it. She was staring at the trees, looking for the familiar shimmer that she had seen the last time.

"Tato?" Sansa kept calling for him, hoping he'd step out so she could say sorry for not being there yesterday. She was starting to feel worried.

What if Tato thought that she had abandoned him?

Maybe he was mad...or sad....

...What if he was hurt..?

Maybe he tried to meet her yesterday and hurt himself! He could be lying in the forest somewhere!!!

...Or.... maybe...

....Maybe...

...He wasn't real...?...

Maybe she had hit her head when she fell into the water and none of it was real.

Tears started to slide down Sansa's cheeks as these thoughts and fears tumbled through her head. She stumbled towards a small group of boulders and sat on one of the flatter rocks, putting her head into her hands, her shoulders shaking as she tried to stop the tears that threatened to fall.

Sansa felt a tap on her shoulder and looked up, blinking at the dark shape blocking out the sun. Tato leaned over and gave her a hug, his arms wrapping around her while the fuzzy moss on his chest brushed roughly against her cheek.

"I'm sorry Tato. I'm so sorry." Sansa sobbed into his chest. Her voice shook with emotion and she felt a lump in her throat. A mix of shame, embarrassment, heartbreak, and sweet relief choked her. "I thought you were mad...or hurt...." Sansa swallowed the knot and whispered raggedly, "I even... thought... you weren't...real...."

Tato held Sansa awkwardly, as though it had been so long since he had tried to comfort anyone. After a few minutes, her tears slowed and she only had the odd hiccup. Sansa pulled away from Tato and wiped her face with a sleeve. She leaned back, looking up at her friend as he straightened.

"I'm sorry I didn't come yesterday. I was mad that I couldn't see you, so I wasn't very nice." Sansa looked down in embarrassment and continued, "And then... I tried to sneak out...."

Sansa knew that if she had waited and not been rude, she might have been able to see Tato. Her parents always told her that she needed to be more patient, and now, because she couldn't wait, she may have hurt someone she cared about.

"Will you please forgive me?" Sansa looked back up at Tato. He smiled somewhat sadly, then nodded.

"It's alright. Come home?"

Sansa climbed off the boulder she had been sitting on, slipping her hand into Tato's before turning towards his home. Tato looked down in surprise, examining her tiny hand in his larger one. He smiled at Sansa, then turned to head to his cave. Sansa realized that she had walked past it earlier, missing the crisscrossing branches and faint, magical shimmer. Once again, as they approached it and were about to enter, the foliage gave way to the large room. As the pair got settled around the fire pit, Sansa remembered her bag.

"I brought you some stuff for your home - and a picnic to share!" Sansa started unpacking the bag and cooler. She kept the food and juice boxes in one of the bags, but placed the blankets, towels, and clothes on what appeared to be shelves made of slabs of rocks. She placed them in neat piles before coming back to gently hand Tato her most treasured friend, Darla.
"I snuggle Darla whenever I'm scared or lonely, and I sleep with her to protect me from bad dreams."

Sansa told him as he looked at her in awe. "I want you to have her now. If I'm not here, she can keep you from feeling sad. And if you feel scared, she'll protect you." Tato looked down at the little dragon in amazement.

No one had ever given him something so important or so well-loved. He felt such joy that his eyes filled as he gazed at Sansa in shock. Sansa saw the tears come to his eyes but misunderstood the cause. She felt her cheeks warm and a sharp stab of disappointment and embarrassment, so she buried her face in Tato's chest as she wrapped her arms around him.

"It's ok!! You don't have to keep her if you don't like her. I just..." Sansa started to reach for Darla, afraid she had upset him, but Tato squeezed Darla to his chest and shook his head at Sansa.

"No!! I will take good care of her. She is precious, like you." Tato pulled Sansa into a tighter hug, Darla squeezed between them. Sansa felt happy tears well up in her eyes, so she held Tato tighter for a for a few more moments.

"I'm glad you like her. Would you like to share that picnic now? We can eat it in here or outside by the water -whatever you want!"

Sansa gave Tato a bashful smile. Who would imagine that this large, green, frightful-looking creature could be so gentle and sensitive? Tato smiled back and stood up to help Sansa.

"By the creek. It's a pretty day to eat outside." Tato replied as he gathered the bags. He took an extra moment to bend over to speak softly to Lasair. Sansa hadn't noticed the small Fire Fae asleep in the glowing embers of the fire pit. Lasair nodded sleepily before closing his eyes again.

Sansa grabbed a blanket from the pile she'd put on his makeshift shelves. Together, they went back outside. It didn't take long to find a dry spot near the water with a fallen tree to sit on and a big, flat rock on which to put their food and drinks. Sansa tore off and opened her straw before poking it into her juice box and taking a big drink. All the walking and crying had made her thirsty.

As Sansa put down the half-empty juice box, her eyes popped open wide, noticing Tato trying to figure out his juice box. He had managed to pull the straw off the side, still wrapped in plastic, but he kept hitting it at the box, not knowing how to make the straw go in. He was frowning at the container, turning and squeezing it in his large hand in confusion. All of a sudden, he squeezed a little too tightly and the juice box burst open, spraying them both with juice!

Sansa and Tato sat frozen for a long moment,

shock written over both their faces, before Sansa started laughing, slapping her hand over her mouth in embarrassment. Tato looked at her, still frowning, before he suddenly burst into deep, bellowing laughs. The laughter seemed to rumble up from his chest, coming out in large, deep notes. Sansa stopped for a moment, surprised by the sound of his deep, booming laughs, then started laughing again. Tato's hummingbird friend flew out of the trees, circling their heads in curiosity before flying away again, seeming to shake it's head in consternation. Sansa and Tato paused as they looked at each other again as the bird flew off in a huff, then started laughing even harder.

The rest of the morning seemed to fly by as they enjoyed the remainder of their picnic, then headed back to Sansa's grandparents' house.

"I'm going to try and come back this afternoon, but if I can't, then tomorrow. I'll see you today or tomorrow, though, I promise!" Sansa gave Tato a squeeze when they stopped a few feet from the edge of the trees. "I promise to try and be good, even if I have to listen and wait."

Sansa stepped out of the trees and was headed to the house when she heard a loud buzzing above her. She looked up, shading her eyes with her hands, and saw looked like a small black helicopter with four propellers holding it up. Sansa looked around but didn't see anyone.  There must be other kids at one of the nearby properties, Sansa thought as she stepped into the house, calling for her Papo and Lita.

"I'm back! Is it lunch time yet?" Sansa called up the stairs. She heard her grandparents chuckle to themselves before calling down.

"We'll be right down. Try not to starve while you wait..." Sansa blushed as she realized how rude she had sounded.

"I'm sorry!! I just meant I wanted to share lunch with you..." Sansa trailed off in embarrassment, but her grandparents came down the stairs, still laughing softly.

"It's okay honey. We knew you weren't trying to be rude." Papo gently ruffled her hair before heading into the kitchen to make lunch.

"Why don't you tell us about your picnic with Darla?" Lita smiled down at Sansa, then put an arm around her shoulders and guided her to the dining room. Sansa smiled up at her grandmother - she couldn't wait to tell her about her picnic. Well, most of it, at least....

6

AFTER SANSA TOLD her grandparents about her picnic - leaving out a few key details about her large, friend - she waited patiently for her grandparents to tell her what their plans would be for the rest of the day. Although she didn't bother them, she just couldn't sit still! Her feet were moving, her fingers were tapping, and her eyes were frequently glancing at the clock. When she thought she couldn't bear it any longer, her Papo finally spoke up.

"So, what do you think Sans'? Want to hang out here this afternoon, maybe play in the woods some more? Or would you like to start building that tree house with me? I think it might be a good day to get started on planning it."

Sansa was uncertain. On the one hand, helping to plan the treehouse might be fun, and she had asked to help. On the other hand, she really, REALLY wanted to go see Tato again - she had so many questions for him.

"Maybe I can help you for a little bit, then play?" Sansa asked eagerly. Papo smiled at her and nodded.

"That sounds like a great idea. We'll go get the plans and figure out where would be a good spot to build it. Then, while I unload all the wood and pieces we need, you can go play. How's that sound?"

"That would be awesome, Papo!!" Sansa jumped up, giving him a big hug, then turned to her Lita and gave her one too. It was perfect!

Papo refilled his juice and grabbed a water bottle for Sansa, before heading out to his truck for the plans. Sansa followed him out and, together, they started walking around the house, looking at trees.

"So we need a good sized tree, plus some close by - enough to help support everything. And we don't want it to be too far from the house, or too close. Hmmm."

Papo started walking into the trees. Sansa continued to follow him, but a flash of movement in the corner of her eye made her pause.

She glanced over, noticing some leaves and branches swaying gently as though brushed by a small breeze. Sansa looked back at her grandfather, but he didn't seem to notice anything. After a few circles around the house, Papo decided on a set of trees that he said 'looked promising'. There was one large tree, surrounded by three smaller trees that were close enough to add the support the treehouse would need. Papo tied some of the orange tape onto the branches of the four trees so he would remember where he wanted to build, then looked over at Sansa with a tender smile.

"Now I get to unload the truck. How strong do you think you are?" Papo asked, looking Sansa up and down.

"I'm not big enough, Papo!" Sansa laughed.

"Show me those muscles!" Papo pointed at Sansa's arms, so she obligingly flexed like she had seen her Dad do in the mirror some mornings. Papo leaned in and squeezed her arms, squinting as though he really was calculating how strong she was.

"Hmmm, you might be right...." Papo shook his head in mock disappointment, a mischievous light in his eyes. "I can help with the smaller stuff!" Sansa exclaimed, slightly offended until she caught the smile playing around his mouth and eyes.

They both started laughing, and Papo picked her up to give her a big hug. He spun her around, Sansa's legs flying out behind her, her happy laughter floating on the wind. After a couple more spins, Papo placed Sansa gently on the ground as her legs wobbled and the world continued to spin for a few more moments.

Once Sansa's legs felt steadier, they walked over to the truck and started unloading it. Papo took the 2x4s, bigger pieces of wood, and metal, while Sansa carried the smaller pieces to where her grandfather was piling everything. It took an extra 20 minutes to help her Papo, but Sansa felt good for helping. As soon as her grandfather told her she was done, she ran towards the woods as he called after her.

"Stay close, stay safe, and be careful!" Sansa turned and waved before stepping into the shadowed forest.

Sansa knew exactly where to go now, so she headed straight for the stream and Tato's home in the mine. She found the entrance to the cave easily and stepped through the shimmering foliage without hesitation.

"Tato!" Sansa called out for her friend as her eyes adjusted to the gloomy cave.

"Sansa!" Tato grinned at her, his bottom fangs shining in the darkness. He was sitting by the fire pit, holding Darla the dragon to his chest as he read aloud from one of his worn books. Lasair was seated near the glowing fire, listening to Tato.

He had put on an old shirt of her grandfather's, although it was too small for his large frame. The long sleeves reached his elbows, and the cuffs were torn where Tato couldn't undo the buttons. He couldn't button the front either, as the shirt wouldn't wrap around him. There appeared to be a tear across the back from where he had tried - and failed - to get the shirt over his shoulders and against the rough texture of his skin. The sweat pants fit a little better, but again, they were too short for him, only reaching his calves.

Sansa looked him over as he stood there, grinning. She thought he looked amazing, still unable to believe that this large, magical creature was her friend. She didn't know what had brought them together, and she didn't care. Sansa grinned back at him and reached out her hand.

"Want to go for a walk in the woods?" Sansa remembered the movement she had noticed in the bushes earlier, "I thought I saw you when I was helping my Papo, but I didn't want him to be worried, so I'm glad you stayed hidden." The troll looked perplexed.

"I was here, waiting for you." Tato placed Darla on the chair so she would be safe, then reached out and took Sansa's hand.

"Huh." Sansa shrugged as they left the cavern, "It must have been an animal or something then."

As Sansa and Tato headed back out into the sunlight and dappled green of the forest, Sansa peppered Tato with questions.

"Tato, why are you here? I mean, I know you said you have to guard a door, but I haven't seen any door, and no one else even knows you're here."

Tato seemed to think about it for a minute before trying to explain. "A long time ago, Fae traveled between worlds, through doorways. They would come and go, in secret. Light Fae, like you... But Dark Fae came, too."

Tato took a deep breath, lost in his memories, before continuing, "The Dark Fae fought the Light Fae - my friends. And bad humans came later."

A look of grief passed over Tato's face, "Many were lost, hurt, or missing. The king sent me, and Lasair, to protect the doorway."

Sansa heard him say good Fae, like her, but thought he meant good people like he thought she was. "What are Fae? Like... fairies? And trolls like you?"

"Lots of Fae. Trolls like Tato, Sprites, Cu-Sith, Centaurs, Duendes, and Hearth Fae like Lasair. All Fae, but all different." Tato tried to explain as they walked, and once they reached a small clearing, he stopped. He kicked aside some leaves and twigs to find the dirt underneath, then found a small stick and drew very rough drawings of

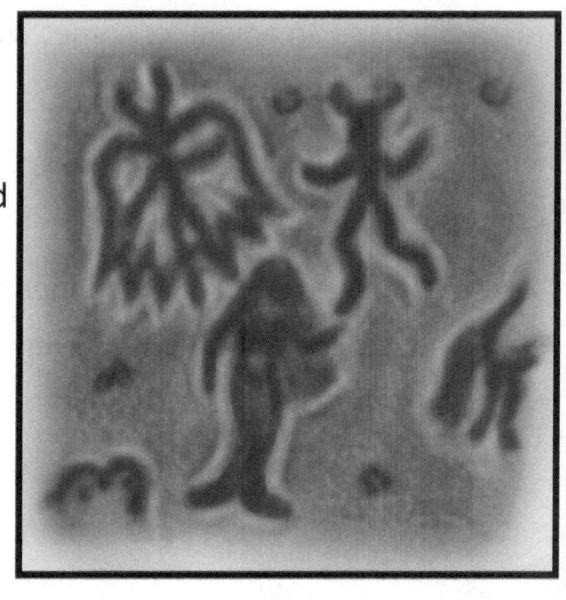

some of the different types of Fae.

"So... why don't we see more Fae? You're the only one I've ever met!" Sansa wondered as she studied the drawings Tato made.

"The doors are closed now. Only Dark Fae can come, and they stay hidden." Tato shook his head sadly.

"How long have you lived here?" Sansa felt tears prick at her eyes as she thought of how much Tato had faced.

Tato stood silently once more, looking up at the trees and sky as Sansa waited for his answer.

"Many upon many moons." Tato shrugged, looking sadly at his young friend..

"Then why stay? Couldn't you open the door again, go back home, and then block the door so no one else could use it?" Sansa couldn't understand why Tato would stay in the woods, living in a cave, alone.

"Only the Royal Family can open the door now, so I wait. Just like my King ordered." Tato looked sadly at Sansa.

"Wait for what?" Sansa wasn't sure why anyone would ask such a kind creature live alone. It seemed like such a cruel punishment.

"For you." Tato said simply.

"Me?!" Sansa looked at Tato in surprise, not sure she heard him right.

Tato smiled at Sansa, nodding his head. "The King said that the magic children will help. You are a magical girl."

Sansa stood staring at her friend, shock written on her face.

"Tato, I'm sorry, but I'm not magic." Sansa told him gently, almost sadly. It would be super cool to have magical abilities, but Sansa knew she didn't. "I'm just a normal person, like everyone else in our world." Sansa stopped, realizing who she was talking to, "Well... except you, of course."Tato continued to smile calmly at Sansa. He didn't say anything else, just reached out to take her hand so they could continue their walk. As they walked hand in hand, Sansa kept thinking about what Tato had said. Not that she was magical - there was no way that could be true - but about the good and bad Fae, and his job to protect the door.

Thinking about the Fae and his mission led her to ask, "Tato, you said there was a door, but I haven't seen one anywhere. Is it magical, too? Like the entrance to your cave?"

Tato nodded and gave Sansa a mischievous smile. He started walking quicker, pulling her along behind him. Sansa started to feel strange as she looked around, and she got the uneasy feeling of butterflies in her stomach. She realized that the trees seemed familiar, but wasn't sure how that could be possible, as she had never been in this part of the woods - then she remembered her dream. She stopped and looked at Tato in shock. "Where are you taking me, Tato?" Sansa asked softly, despite being sure she already knew the answer.

"You will see." As he spoke, he tugged on her hand again, pulling her out of the trees and into a clearing. Sure enough, just like in her dream, Sansa could see the hills and woods spread down around them. They stood at the top of a

hill with a valley stretched across the horizon. Sansa turned in a circle, eyes wide, seeing everything from her dream. As the shock wore off, Sansa felt amazed and humbled. She looked at Tato with awe.

"I dreamt about this!" Sansa said in surprise. She flung her arms out, looking around the clearing and hills again.

Tato smiled down at her, then looked up and pointed across the clearing. Sansa looked over to where he pointed and gasped in shock. Across from them stood the largest, most magnificent tree she had ever seen. It was exactly how she remembered it from her dream, yet somehow... more. It must have been as tall as a ten story building, its branches seeming to twist and writhe

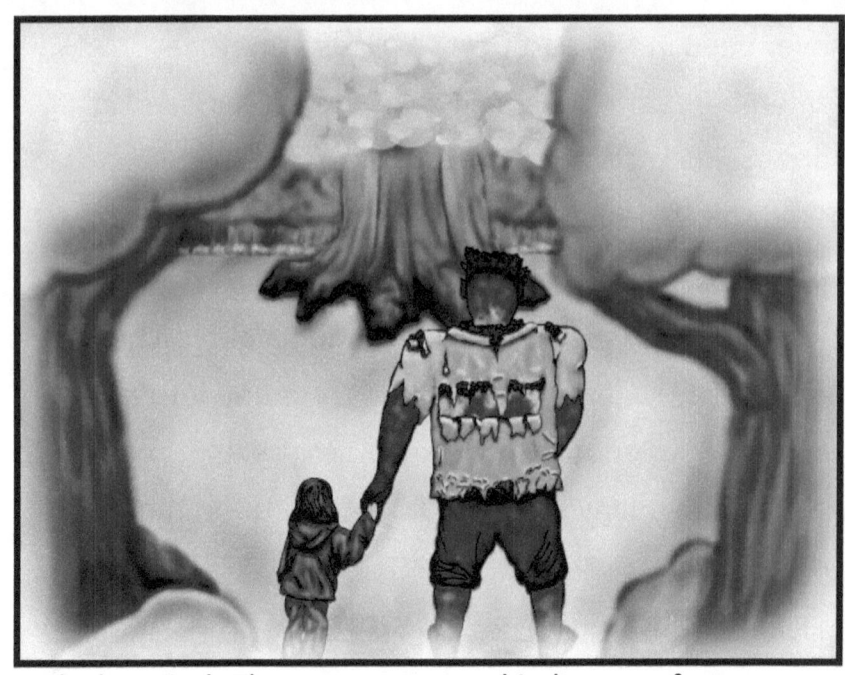

with the wind. They were covered in leaves of every color, and the trunk was so wide that she couldn't see around it. The feeling of magic surrounded the tree, and the air seemed to shimmer the same as the entrance to Tato's home in the mine. Although Sansa couldn't see a doorway like she had in her dream, the texture of the bark seemed to form a rough shadow of an archway. Even the birds were silent, respectful of the sacred site.

"Tato, this is...amazing." Sansa was practically speechless, her eyes wide and her face alight in wonder.

"Home." Tato said simply, but as he stared at the tree, Sansa could see a mix of emotions sweeping over his face. There was joy at seeing the doorway home, sadness for his lost family, and hope that he may soon be able to return home. Sansa reached for his hand, squeezing it gently. "We'll get you home, Tato. I promise."

They stood there in silence, the giant troll and the small girl, staring at the tree, each lost in their own thoughts.

7

SANSA SPENT ANOTHER hour or so walking through the woods with Tato, before she soon realized it was time to head home or her Papo and Lita might start worrying. She still couldn't believe what Tato had told her about the Fae realm, but when she closed her eyes, she could picture the large castle he had described. It was made of pink stone surrounded by rolling hills of giant trees, like the magical one Tato took her too. The castle was located on an island, with mountains, waterfalls, and forests surrounding and protecting it. Many different types of Fae have lived on the island, and in the nearby Light Fae lands, including Tato's family who used to live in caves at the base of the mountains.

Sansa was so lost in thought, imagining this magical realm and thinking about how to get Tato home, that she didn't realize how close to her grandparents' house they had come.

As they reached the edge of the trees by the house, Sansa looked up in surprise before turning to Tato, giving him a halfhearted hug, her mind still lost in the Light Fae realm.

"I'll come see you as soon as I can, ok? I'm not sure what my grandparents want to do tomorrow, but as soon as I'm allowed, I'll come to the mine." Tato nodded and smiled at Sansa as she turned to run to the house.

She stopped just before stepping out from the shadow of the trees, turning to watch Tato. He was already headed home, ducking beneath low branches and shuffling carefully through the trees. Once he was out of sight, Sansa turned back and stepped into the sunlight. She had only taken a few steps when she noticed the dark car in the driveway. It was black, similar to her parent's car, but the windows were tinted and a strange picture was painted on the door. As Sansa approached the car, she could make out the logo on the door - it depicted a large tree with it's roots and branches intertwined, much like the doorway Tato had shown her earlier. However, instead of a doorway in the center of the tree trunk, there was an open eye. The eye seemed to be staring straight at

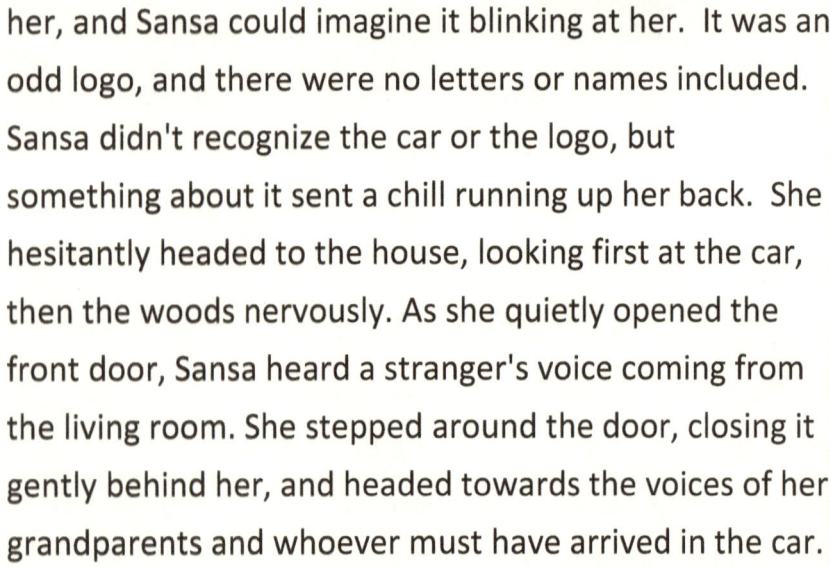

her, and Sansa could imagine it blinking at her. It was an odd logo, and there were no letters or names included. Sansa didn't recognize the car or the logo, but something about it sent a chill running up her back. She hesitantly headed to the house, looking first at the car, then the woods nervously. As she quietly opened the front door, Sansa heard a stranger's voice coming from the living room. She stepped around the door, closing it gently behind her, and headed towards the voices of her grandparents and whoever must have arrived in the car.

"Sansa! Oh, thank goodness you're ok!" Lita jumped up off the couch the moment she spotted her granddaughter, running to wrap her arms around Sansa.

"Of course I am. I was just out playing." Sansa looked at her grandmother in confusion - why would Lita be worried about her? She had been playing in the woods all week. Although she said nothing, her grandfather seemed to understand her questioning glance and stood up, gesturing to the man sitting on the couch.

"Sansa, this is Dr. Birch. He's with the Wildlife Protection Institute and has been visiting local homes about a wild animal in the region."

Sansa looked over at the man, immediately feeling uncomfortable. Dr. Birch studied her, squinting slightly, as if trying to understand something unseen. His eyes were direct and probing, an icy blue behind a pair of dark, silver framed glasses. He wore a dark suit with a white shirt and dark tie, shiny black shoes, and looked more like a banker than a doctor. His dark hair was combed back from his forehead with streaks of silver at his temples. His eyes crinkled at the corners, although they did not warm even as he smiled at Sansa. The satisfied smirk sent chills down Sansa's back as she thought Dr. Birch looked just like a cat who caught a mouse.

"Yes, hello young lady. I have come to your grandparent's home, and neighboring houses, because we have received calls about some kind of wild animal in the region. I'm trying to gather more information as we visit locals to warn them not to wander into the woods." He looked Sansa up and down with a small smile on his face. "I hear you like to play in the woods around the house. I'm glad to see you're safe and would advise you not to play there anymore until this... creature has been captured.

"Sansa's skin crawled at his meaningful pause, and she shivered when she thought of what he meant by "captured".

"I've been staying close, but I haven't seen anything, sir." Sansa looked down at her toes, uncomfortable with both lying and making eye contact with Dr. Birch. She felt like he could see through her lie.

"Well, I'm glad to hear that... you're sure you haven't heard anything strange while playing? The creature may look innocent, but it is nothing but a wild, lost animal. It cares nothing for you." Dr. Birch leaned forward avidly, his eyes lit with something dark that Sansa could neither place nor understand as she hesitantly looked up at him.

"No sir, I... Um, I haven't seen anything un-unusual. Umm, what kind of...animal...is it?" Sansa looked back down at her toes, stuttering over her words. All she could think about now was that this strange man could not know about Tato.

Dr. Birch sat back, staring at Sansa knowingly, as if he knew she was lying. "Well, I'm not exactly certain yet. It sounds like it may be a mountain lion or a lost bear. Regardless, until it is caught, stay out of the woods." He turned his gaze away from Sansa and to her grandparents, allowing Sansa a small sigh of relief."There will be some agents coming to search for, and hopefully capture, this creature before it hurts anyone. I'd suggest you keep your granddaughter safe indoors with you... I would hate for anything to happen to this sweet young lady."

Although Sansa's grandparents didn't seem to notice, she was certain that the last sentence was meant as a threat. She looked up to find the doctor's cold eyes staring at her again. Sansa shivered, as though the ice in his eyes had frozen the blood in her veins. She stepped closer to her grandmother, causing Lita to look at her in surprise before looking back at their visitor.

"We will definitely keep her close. Thank you for taking the time to come and warn us. I'm sorry we don't have more information, but I hope you can capture it quickly and safely!"

Dr. Birch stood up, inclining his head to the three of them. "Well, I must head to the next house to inform them as well. You have my card, so if you do happen to see anything unusual, please do not hesitate to reach out to myself or my colleagues."

Papo and the doctor headed outside as Lita looked at Sansa. "You're looking a little dirty from playing... Why don't you head upstairs to wash up and change into some clean clothes?"

Sansa nodded and ran upstairs, but before doing what Lita asked, she hurried to her bed and peeked out the window above it. She knew Papo was waiting for the strange Doctor to leave, but she expected the car would already be turning to head down the driveway. However, as she pushed the curtain aside, Sansa gasped. She quickly drew back, her heart pounding, when she saw Dr. Birch staring up at her window. Sansa knew something was wrong - she suspected Tato was the "creature" the doctor was talking about. Sansa knew she needed to warn Tato that he was in danger.

After dinner that night, Sansa excused herself to play upstairs rather than spending the evening watching TV with her grandparents. Once upstairs, instead of playing, Sansa began making plans. She needed to find a way to warn Tato about the strange man and his organization, but she also needed to find a way to get him home before anyone else found him. Sansa knew she had to do this without her grandparents and the strange doctor finding out, making it that much harder.

Sansa started gathering warm clothes, her jacket, and a flashlight, putting them together on her bed. She knew she

should talk to her grandparents before doing anything crazy, but she couldn't risk them not believing her, trying to stop her, or possibly even calling Dr. Birch about Tato. Sansa was trying to protect Tato, and she was certain that they would understand that if they ever found out. Once she had found everything she needed, Sansa folded it all into a pillowcase, tucked it under a couple of cushions in the corner, and headed downstairs.

Sansa spent the rest of the evening with her Lita, watching TV until bed time. After her grandparents tucked her in, Sansa lay in the dark, listening and waiting for them to head to bed, only managing to avoid falling asleep by thinking about the danger Tato was in. Eventually, when the moon was shining brightly into her room, Sansa heard nothing but silence. She had listened to her grandparents getting ready for bed about an hour earlier, so she was certain that they would both be asleep already.

Sansa quietly climbed out of bed, arranging the pillows and pulling the blankets over them in case her grandparents decided to check on her. She dressed in her warm clothes, pulled on her jacket, and tiptoed down the stairs, keeping her flashlight off. She put her shoes on quickly, then made her way to the front door. Before opening it, she stopped to listen again, only hearing her Papo's snores and the quiet mumble of the TV in her grandparent's room. Sansa slowly unlocked and opened the door. As she stepped outside, she froze, thinking she'd heard a footstep off to the side of the house. After a moment, when she didn't hear anything else, she moved again, closing the door silently behind her.

Sansa turned on the flashlight, carefully pointing it straight at the ground so that the light wouldn't give her away. She quickly headed to the trees, trying to keep the light pointed away from the house. Once she was a few feet into the woods, Sansa started pointing the flashlight at the trees, looking for her orange tape. The darkness made it hard to get a good sense of direction, so Sansa was worried she might get lost. As soon as she spotted the first of her pieces of tape, she breathed a sigh of relief and started following the trail, remaining as quiet as possible. Knowing how sound would carry on the quiet night air, Sansa stepped as lightly as possible on small patches of clear grass. When she couldn't see anything, she slowed so as to limit the crunching of dead leaves or branches underfoot. Every few minutes, she would stop and listen. When she didn't hear anything other than the rustle of leaves in the light breeze, she continued on. Finally, she came upon the creek and headed upstream to the mine entrance. As she approached Tato's home, Sansa started calling his name softly.

"Tato...." The silence of the woods around them was eerie as a cloud passed over the moon making the darkness seem closer. Sansa didn't feel like she was in the same woods she had been playing in for the past few days. Even when she had been lost, the forest had felt welcoming. Now it felt cold and dangerous.

"Tato?" Sansa called out again as she stepped up to the entrance of his home. The foliage shimmered gently as she stepped through, looking over her shoulder one last time.

Thankfully, Tato had a fire smoldering in the fire

pit, giving off some light in the darkness. Sansa could see Tato sitting by the fire, Darla in his arms, and Lasair on his nearby stone. They both looked up in surprise when Sansa stepped in, Tato's face quickly lighting up as he recognized her.

"Sansa!" He called as he stood up, excited to see her so soon, but the smile faded as a look of confusion passed over his face. "You okay?"

"I'm alright, Tato, but I don't think you are!" Sansa told her troll friend, and the Flame Faeling, about the strange man who had been waiting at home when she had returned earlier. "I think he's looking for you...."

Tato heard the fear in her voice, and realized that the enemy had found him at last. He didn't question her feelings or fears - he had been waiting for this day...dreading it. Tato sadly looked around the home he'd known for so long.

"Tato, I need to know.... Can you go home? Will the door work? Is it safe?" Sansa needed her friend to be safe.

"I don't know. They are sealed until the blood returns. I have to wait -" Tato was interrupted by a booming sound outside. Sansa ran to the entrance, peering out into the darkness between branches. She couldn't see anything in the gloom, but her heart was racing.

"We need to go! It's not safe for you here anymore." Sansa had turned back to Tato, putting her back to the branches covering the entrance. Suddenly, the room was lit from behind Sansa, bright lights stretching Sansa's shadow up the far wall of the cave. Sansa and Tato froze, looking at each other in fear.

"Oh no...*they found us*."

8

SANSA, TATO, AND Lasair stood staring at each other, the light seeming to sway back and forth as they noticed the chopping of a helicopter outside.

"It's not too late, Tato - but we need to run!" Sansa grabbed Tato by the hand, waiting for him to pick up Lasair before stepping through the foliage and into the bright light.

They were momentarily blinded by the spotlight shining down from the helicopter that hovered above their heads, lighting the entire area around the mouth of the mine and the creek. Sansa looked around them, trying to find a safe place to run. She could hear rushing feet in the brush off to their side, coming from the direction of her grandparent's house.

"Across the stream, Tato - can you carry both of us?" Sansa turned to her large friend, pointing into the trees opposite the sound of rustling and the stomping of heavy boots.

Tato didn't hesitate, picking Sansa up and putting her on his left shoulder as Lasair climbed onto his other shoulder. Tato then jumped across the large boulders protruding from the creek, before racing into the trees. As they rushed through the trees, Tato ducked low beneath branches and leaves, trying to keep his passengers steady and unharmed. The helicopter attempted to follow them, the light swinging back and forth around them, but the foliage above was too dense to pinpoint their location. As they ran, Sansa could hear the stomping and crackling behind them. She tried to look behind, hoping to see how close they were, but it was too gloomy in the trees to see anything.

"Tato, what are we going to do?" Sansa's voice was shaking, her heart racing, and tears were starting to run down her cheeks. "I'm scared Tato - they can't find you!" She wrapped her arms around Tato's neck, squeezing as she buried her face in his neck.

"It will be alright, we will keep you safe."

Tato reached up and handed Darla to Sansa. She hadn't realized he had brought the little dragon.

"How...?" Sansa blinked at the troll as she freed an arm to hug her stuffed dragon.

Tato spared her a quick glance and a lopsided smile as he chuckled. "Pockets are perfect for small friends."

Tato looked ahead again, continuing to run and dodge trees. Sansa noticed the sounds of those behind them seemed to fall away. Tato gradually slowed, taking a deep breath as he looked around. Sansa was surprised that he didn't seem out of breath after all the running. As he came to a stop, the troll gently took Sansa off his shoulder and placed her on a wide branch about ten feet off the ground. He then knelt down so Lasair could leap off.

"Lasair and I will go and look around. You stay safe up here. Wait for us." Sansa grabbed hold of the trunk, nodding tearfully at Tato as she tucked Darla under her shirt.

"Be careful, please..." Tato nodded in response, then stepped off into the shadows. Lasair watched the troll for a moment, wanting to follow his old friend. He then shook his head and turned to walk in the opposite direction, dimming his light as he disappeared into the brush.

Sansa was too scared to question why the leaves and branches didn't catch fire as the small Fire Fae walked through them, but given that he was Fae and Magical, she would have assumed he was able to control the fire. Instead, Sansa listened carefully, trying to detect any sound that might give away their pursuers. She couldn't hear anything, not even the reassuring sounds of birds, owls, or  other forest animals, just her heart thundering in her ears. As she strained her eyes to see something, anything, in the darkness, two figures stepped out of the trees below her. Sansa's heart dropped to her stomach and she slapped her hand across her mouth to smother the gasp that escaped her lips. She quietly pulled her legs in as close as she could, perching on the branch and hugging the tree in the hope that they wouldn't see her.

After a few long minutes, a loud crack came from just off to the side of the tree Sansa hid in. The sound of a scuffle and a few grunts and groans followed. The men below Sansa ran off towards the sound, leaving the little girl hidden in the tree. Sansa started chewing her bottom lip, unsure of what to do; Tato had told her to wait, but he might be in danger!

She sat quietly for another minute, but when a cry sounded out, Sansa knew she needed to act. Although she began to carefully climb down from the tree, there were no branches below her hiding place, forcing her to hang off the branch with her arms, then let go and drop to the ground. As she was holding on, preparing to drop, someone grabbed her from behind. Sansa's heart stopped, even as she hoped it was Tato who had grabbed her - but her hopes were quickly crushed by the sly voice whispering in her ear.

"I knew you would help us track this thing down." Dr. Birch stressed the word "thing" as if even mentioning the troll was foul.

"I'm not going to help you!" Sansa answered him

defiantly before taking a deep breath, preparing to yell for Tato to run. Dr. Birch seemed to realize her plan and dropped her heavily on the ground, causing her to lose her breath and effectively stopping her from yelling.

"Don't worry, dear. You'll be able to call for your friend - when I'm ready." Sansa hated the way his hot breath washed over her face as he bent over her. He smirked at her attempts to regulate her breathing again before giving three sharp whistles. After a few moments, two figures stumbled out of the brush, one limping as they approached.

"It got away, Doctor," The one with the limp told Dr. Birch somberly. "It also knocked out a few members of the team - but I tagged it with the tranquilizer. It won't get far."

"Perfect! You, keep tracking it." Birch told the uninjured agent. As the first agent jogged off, Birch turned to the second. "Radio the chopper and get the agents back to the creek. We can regroup there and use our bait to catch our prey. For now, make yourself useful and carry the girl." Dr. Birch stepped back as the agent limped over to carefully kneel down where Sansa sat on the ground, "And agent? Don't disappoint me again."

Sansa watched the man's face pale as he paused

and nodded. He quickly resumed tying her hands behind her back and her feet together before slinging her over his shoulder. The three of them started towards the creek, but Dr. Birch stopped somewhat suddenly, took off his tie, and tied it around Sansa's mouth to gag her.

"Can't have you warning our friend before we're ready for him, now can we?" Dr. Birch smiled at Sansa, but his eyes remained ice cold and full of hate.

They set off again, Sansa bouncing on the shoulder of the injured agent as he limped behind Dr. Birch. It didn't take long for the small group to reach the creek, where seven other agents and the helicopter waited for them. The agent carrying Sansa dropped her down on the rocky shore, causing Darla to fall out from under her shirt. The agent didn't notice the little stuffed dragon or Sansa's cry of pain, muffled by the gag, focused instead on tying the girl to a tree by the rocks so she couldn't escape. Tears were running down Sansa's face as the reality of what was happening hit her. She should have listened to Tato when he told her to wait. Why couldn't she ever be patient and stay put? Now, her friend was going to be captured by these horrible men, all because she couldn't wait...

Dr. Birch started giving orders to the agents,

directing them up and down the stream, setting his trap for Tato. After sending his men to their hiding places nearby, Dr. Birch stalked over to Sansa and crouched down to take the gag off. "Before we capture this creature, I have to ask. Why would you befriend something as hideous as this monster?"

Sansa sniffled, thinking about her friend. She remembered everything they'd seen and done in their short time together: how he had saved her from the rushing water and sharp rocks; the way he had helped her find her way after getting lost in the woods, how tightly he had hugged Darla when she gave her to him; the tears and sadness in his eyes when she had let him down; the joy on his face when he showed her the door to his home; and when he had shared what little he had with her. Tato may not have been human, and he may not have been like anyone she had ever met, or known, but he was beautiful to her. The love, trust, friendship, and caring he had shown to her in the short time they had known each other meant more to her than she could have imagined. The truth hit her then. She could save Tato. She WOULD save Tato! He was not the monster Dr. Birch kept talking about.

"I won't let you capture him. He's not a monster,

you are! He is kind and gentle, and I will do anything to save him from you!" Sansa told Dr. Birch.

"You know nothing, little girl. He is nothing but a misplaced monster from a realm filled with equally monstrous creatures - beings from his land care nothing for the people from ours. The only thing his kind are good for is to keep us strong. You will help us, whether or not you want to." Dr. Birch stood and turned to call out into the woods around them.

"I know you can hear me! I have your little friend, and if you want her to stay safe, you had better show yourself!" Dr. Birch turned in a slow circle, calling out to the forest surrounding them.

"Tato, no!! Don't listen to him, stay hidden!" Sansa couldn't help calling out a warning.

The silence was heavy, as if the night held it's breath and the forest residents watched and waited. Sansa thought she saw a flicker of light out of the corner of her eye, but it disappeared before she could focus on it. Finally, there was a rustling from behind Sansa, and she felt a short tug on the ropes around her wrists.

Tato stepped out from behind the tree, growling at the humans.

"Let her go."

9

"TATO, NO..." SANSA whispered quietly, tears falling as she stared up at Tato in horror.

Before she could take another breath, the helicopter turned, pointing its spotlight on Tato as the agents rushed in from the surrounding brush. Tato staggered as he tried to back away from the group, the tranquilizer in his shoulder dulling each movement. The men surrounded him as Dr. Birch stood back, a nasty smirk on his face. As the men closed in on Tato, they pulled out what looked to be short-barreled guns and pointed them at the troll. As they fired, Sansa realized that it wasn't guns they held, but tasers instead.

They were shooting small darts into the troll. Still, she screamed as he fell before her, tugging on the ropes that tied her to the trees. As her hands pulled free, Sansa realized the pulling she had felt earlier was Tato, undoing the restraints.

As tears blurred the world around her, and with a heavy heart, Sansa resisted running to Tato, instead slowly moving around and behind the tree she had been tied to. Her toe caught on something, and Sansa looked down, spotting Darla on the ground at her feet. She bent over, picking Darla up and dusting her off, then tucking her back under her sweater. She then peeked around the tree and saw Tato looking at her through eyes glazed over with pain.

"I will save you, Tato. I promise," she whispered.

Sansa was about to step back into the shadows, when she saw Tato stand up, his knees weak and wobbling. Her heart seemed to stop as she watched him brush the darts aside as if they were nothing before roaring at the surrounding agents. They stumbled back in a mix of shock and fear, and even Dr. Birch seemed taken aback. That moment was Tato needed, allowing him to dash forward, grab Sansa from behind the tree, and run into the woods once again.

"Tato! Are you ok? Where are we going to go?"

Sansa whispered the words into his ear, the knot still in her throat. She tightened her arms around his neck, her heart still thundering in her chest. He looked down at her, a wan smile on his face. Her friend looked so tired and in such pain, but still he didn't stop. From behind them, they could hear the shouts and stomping as the agents chased after them in the woods. Ahead, a light flickered in the distance, guiding them.

"Home. Time to go home." Tato said sadly, his voice ragged.

Sansa knew then that he was heading for the doorway to his land. His time living in these woods was at an end, and she would never see him again. Sansa swallowed the tears, knowing it was what was best for him. She wanted him to be safe, and the Light Fae Realm was the only place he would be.

"Let's get you home then...." Sansa took a deep breath, then gave Tato the bravest smile she could muster.

She looked around as Tato ran, the forest quiet and dark around them. Sansa noticed it was getting brighter ahead of them, and she feared that the helicopter would be waiting for them. Before she could say anything in warning, Sansa saw a break in the trees ahead of them, and a few moments later, Tato charged into the field near the magic tree. The meadow was lit from the small flame creature waiting for them. Lasair stood a few feet away, glowing brightly to help them find their way. He smiled at Sansa before turning to his friend. Tato had dropped to his knees, trying to place Sansa on the ground as gently as possible. Sansa released her arms and jumped out of his a moment before he collapsed at her feet.

"Tato! You need to get up! We're almost there." Sansa tried to help Tato stand, pulling at his arm. She quickly realized that she wasn't strong enough. Lasair must have realized that too as he ran to Tato's other arm and draped it over his shoulder. The flames didn't appear to burn or bother the troll, and Sansa was certain that the two of them would be able to get their friend to his feet. She glanced back to the woods behind them, hearing the agents closing in on them. She knelt down, putting her head close to Tato's and whispering urgently into his ear.

"Tato, I know you can do this. Lasair and I believe in you and your strength. We need you to get up. NOW!"

Tato heard her through the fog of pain and knew

what he needed to do. He stubbornly pushed to his knees, using the strength of his friends to leverage himself up to his feet. He stumbled clumsily before finding his balance, his companions supporting him on either side. They slowly set off towards the large tree, crossing the open field. The three could hear the agents closing in on them, rushing out of the trees behind them. They tried to pick up speed, knowing they couldn't outrun the trained agents. A bright beam surrounded the three, blinding them long enough for the agents to catch up and surround the group, Dr. Birch sauntering up last.

"Tato, you need to run." Sansa tried pushing him towards the tree but he wouldn't leave her side.

Sansa looked desperately at Lasair, hoping the Hearth Fae would help Tato escape. He only shook his head at her, confirming her suspicion that he would not abandon her either. Tato stumbled, falling back to his knees, pulling Sansa down with him. Lasair managed to regain his balance and cautiously watched as the agents quickly closed in on the trio. They pointed their tasers at both Tato and Lasair, as the helicopter hovered above them, highlighting the entire area. Sansa looked at the tree in desperation.

"There's no one to help you now." Dr. Birch said with glee. He looked at the agents around him, then looked down at Tato, Sansa, and finally, Lasair. "What's this? Another sample for us! Won't be our first of it's kind, but mustn't look a gift horse in the mouth. Ha!"

They drew closer to Sansa, Lasair, and Tato, hard eyes steady as the agents prepared to attack. Everything seemed to slow down as Sansa looked over at the tree again. Her eyes widened as she noticed the shimmering light surrounding the leaves. No, the light was coming from the leaves, and from the outline of a door in the trunk of the tree. Her dream...

For the first time that night, Sansa felt hope bloom in her chest. She knew what to do, but there was only one chance and Sansa had to wait for the right moment. She pushed herself to her knees, sitting back on her heels as Tato regained his balance. She looked up at the men around them, tears shining on her face.

"How could you?" She demanded of the men around her. "Tato is a sweet, kind creature - he wouldn't hurt any one of you - if you hadn't attacked him first! You're all more monstrous than he is."

The hard faces of the men stared down at her, a mix of pity and hatred in their eyes.

"I said to take it down - now!" Dr. Birch's face was ugly in the harsh light of the helicopter, the angles of his face sharpening. His face appeared to ripple, as if there were snakes under his skin. No one but Sansa seemed to notice, and it confirmed something she had suspected all along - Birch was the true creature - something no longer human. Whatever was going on with the doctor, and the agency he worked for, Sansa was sure they were hurting the Fae to do something to themselves.

The men turned back to Tato and aimed their tasers. However, no one had noticed that Lasair had been mumbling quietly under his breath. As the agents prepared to squeeze their triggers, the fire Faeling split into eight smaller flames. They were all knee high, but as they quickly formed a tight circle around the three friends, their combined flames flared into the night sky, blinding the attacking humans. Lasair and Sansa pushed up with Tato's shoulders, helping him to regain his feet. The small rest seemed to help some of the effects of the tranquilizer to wear off, giving the troll enough strength to pick up his speed. The fire Faelings cleared a path so the three could charge towards the tree. The agents rubbed at their eyes, blind to where their prey had run. The helicopter pilot must have also been blinded as well, as the spotlight didn't follow them.

When Lasair, Tato, and Sansa were only a few steps from the tree, Sansa heard heavy footsteps behind her. She didn't allow herself the luxury of looking over her shoulder, fearful that she would trip or slow down if she looked away from her target the tree. She now knew what she had to do. The tree had shown her the true strength of her blood. She was one of The Children, and she would save her friend.

The tree seemed to brighten as she neared it, the doorway even more visible in the trunk of the giant tree as rainbow light seeped out from the leaves and branches. She paused, looking up as the tree shimmered and started shining even brighter, as the shimmer became an outpouring of multicolored light. Sansa stopped at the base of the tree, awestruck as she reached out her hand to lay it on the trunk at the center of the doorway. She felt a hand grab for her, the briefest brush against her shoulder, before a giant flash of light burst from the trunk.

Magic rolled out of the tree, knocking Sansa back a step and momentarily blinding her. As she blinked, the light faded to a soft glow, and Sansa looked around her, taking in the aftermath of the tree opening. Tato and Lasair stood together, looking at Sansa in shock, the

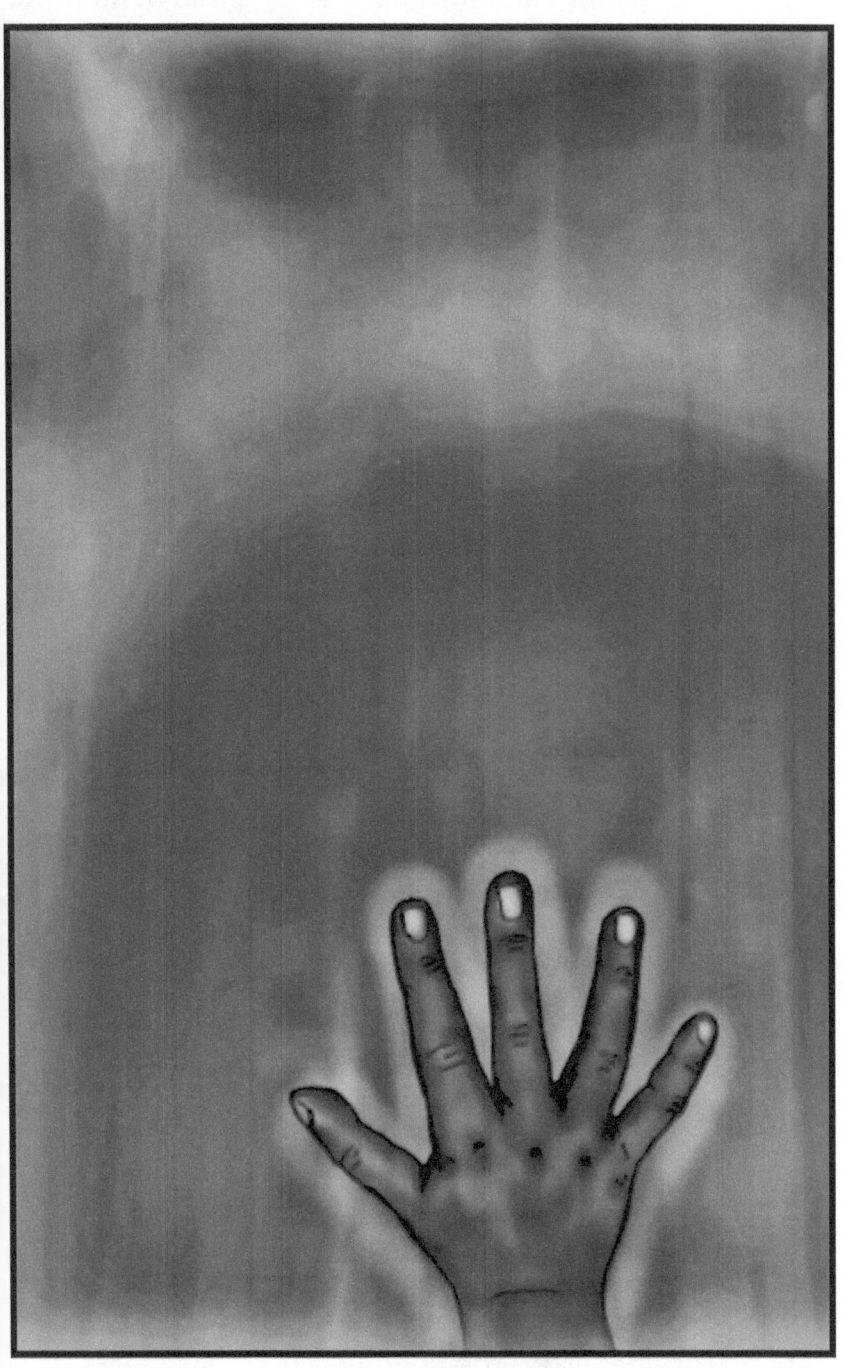

smaller fire Faelings still forming a semi-circle behind the group. The agents were laying on their backs, silent and motionless. The helicopter must have been knocked back as well, the spotlight swinging wildly across the terrain as the pilot attempted to regain control.

Sansa couldn't see Dr. Birch anywhere, but didn't want to wait around trying to find him. She stepped back to Tato, slipping under his arm to help him though the now open door. Lasair paused at the doorway, just as Tato did for him decades ago. The smaller fire Faelings made their way to Lasair, melding and rejoining until he was one single Flame Fae again. Sansa's head shot up as she heard a faint groan from where the agents lay.

"We have to hurry. Before they wake up."

The three stepped the rest of the way through the portal, and Sansa noticed a smear of something dark and forbidding just a few feet away. She thought that was where she had been standing when her hand touched the trunk and opened the door.... Could that have been Dr. Birch? Sansa started to turn back to investigate when she felt a sharp tug on her arm and a bright, white light grew until she was blinded. Unable to see where she was going, Sansa trusted her two companions as she stepped forward - into the unknown.

SANSA STOOD STILL, blinking as she was blinded by the bright light she, Tato, and Lasair had stepped into. As her vision returned, she looked around, surprised to see that it was no longer night. The sky above them was washed in beautiful shades of blue, purple, and pink, spotted with a few bright white clouds as the sun shone down on her, Lasair, and Tato. They stood in the middle of a forest again, but the trees were different from the ones by her grandparents' house. They were taller than any trees she had seen before, with beautiful, twisting branches and multicolored leaves. Sansa could hear the birds singing in the trees and rustling in the bushes around them. She even thought she saw tiny eyes peeking out of the foliage closest to them, but when she blinked, they were gone.

"Tato? Where are we?" Sansa whispered softly, her eyes wide as she looked around in awe.

"Home," He said simply, grinning down at her even as he tightly held her hand.

Sansa was speechless. This was the Fae realm? Tato and Lasair's home? It was magical, and beautiful, and amazing.

"Why is it daytime?" Sansa wondered aloud.

"Time moves differently here." Tato took a moment to get his bearings. The three friends stood together a moment longer before the large troll started heading into the trees, Sansa and Lasair following him.

"Tato, wait! I don't want to get lost!!" Sansa wasn't sure how she was going to get home, but if she got lost in these woods, she was certain she'd never find her way back.

"I know this forest, I won't let you get lost." Tato smiled over his shoulder, his face alight. Sansa couldn't imagine how he felt, being back in his woods after all those years. Seeing the joy in his eyes, she smiled back, knowing he would be true to his word and help her home.

Before they headed deeper into the woods, Sansa took one last glance over her shoulder, back to where they had arrived. She saw two giant trees whose branches had woven together to form a shimmering archway. Sansa realized it was the Fae side of the portal home. Looking ahead once more, she was amazed at how bright everything was. Long, sparkling beams of light penetrated the leaves above them, and even the air smelled different here - pure and clear.

After walking for a few minutes, Sansa realized she could hear the sound of running water. A few more steps brought the three friends out of the woods and into a small clearing. There, she saw two pools of water, both feeding into a large waterfall that tumbled down into the sea below. Sansa gasped as she looked down at the most beautiful waterfall she had ever seen. The drops seemed to freeze in midair, sparkling in the light, and the cascading water was a liquid rainbow, all colors shimmering and shining. It looked as though it was made of pure magic. Tato stopped at the edge of the lower pool, and looked down at Sansa, Lasair still watching the water in awe, amazed he was home again.

"Would you like to sit?" Tato asked her gently. Sansa simply nodded, speechless. They quickly found a few small boulders to sit on, and Sansa took off her shoes and socks to

dangle her feet in the water. It felt refreshingly cool and soft against her toes as the three sat silently, each lost in their own thoughts.

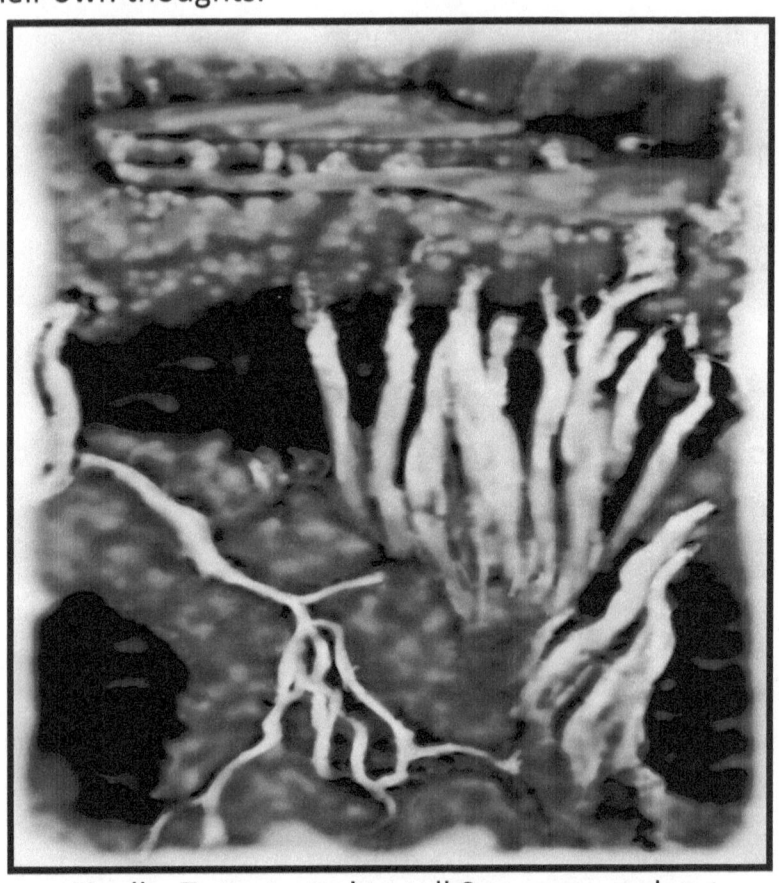

Finally, Tato started to tell Sansa more about growing up in the Fae realm, with Lasair either nodding or correcting Tato in his soft, crackling voice. Tato pointed in different directions, describing the lands where he was raised and fought for his king and home.

He painted a picture of the lands surrounding the mountains on this small island off the coast of the main Fae Continent. This island was the home of the Royal family, and consisted of forests, fields, the mountains, and this magical waterfall, known as *An Tuar Ceatha*. Although they couldn't see it, Tato pointed in the direction of where the castle stood, it's spires tall and graceful, the pink stone shimmering in the sunlight.

Tato also told Sansa about his time as a Royal Guard, which was how he came to know the king. He and Lasair shared many adventures during Tato's time as a personal guard for the princess. After she left the realm, Tato remained as a Royal Guard and personal friend to the king, until he found a new assignment for the troll. The king needed a Guardian in the human realm and only the bravest and truest Guard would be selected. Tato and Lasair were both proud that he was chosen to be a Guardian of the Doorway, as it was an honor to live in the other realm, not a punishment as Sansa had feared.

Sansa shared her own stories with Tato and Lasair, describing what it was like growing up with sisters in the Human Realm. She told him about how smart Katie was, and how proud Sansa was of her big sister. They laughed as she told Tato about some of Bella's crazier adventures, and how much Sansa hoped she would be as brave as her middle sister. Then she told him about how she finally learned to be patient, thanks to him. As Sansa's voice faded to silence, the trio sat quietly, watching the soaring birds and listening to the falling water.

"I will see you again, Tato. I will wait and be patient, but I will find a way to see you again. Until then..." Sansa pulled Darla out from under her shirt, where the little dragon had been tucked. "Take care of Darla for me, ok?"

Tato gently took Darla from Sansa and nodded.

"I have to go back now, Tato." She whispered bravely over the lump in her throat. Tato nodded solemnly, his eyes serious.

"Will it be safe, do you think? Or will the doctor and his agents be waiting?" Sansa didn't know what to expect when she went back through the portal. She didn't know if it would be the next day by now, or still night. Had her grandparents found out she had snuck out? Sansa hoped not; she didn't want to worry them - or her parents.

"Time is different here. We will look before you

go, right Lasair?" Tato smiled down at both of his friends. Sansa smiled softly and looked down at her hand, still wrapped in Tato's. Tato stood and helped Sansa dry her feet on some nearby moss before putting on her shoes and socks. The three friends slowly headed back into the trees, Tato leading them to the archway. Sansa was saddened to be leaving Tato, worried that the portal would be sealed forever once she went through. To distract herself, Sansa began sharing some of her favorite memories of meeting Tato and Lasair. They all laughed as Sansa remembered being picked up into the air at the creek. Tato talked about trying to help her out of the forest when she had been lost. Too quickly, they reached the two large trees, the archway shimmering still beneath the intertwined branches. They paused a few feet from the portal, each taking a deep breath before stepping through, together. This time, Sansa was better prepared for the bright light and wasn't as blinded when she stepped into the clearing.

Tato and Lasair looked around quickly, but there was no sign of the agents. The only sound that could be heard was a far off owl and the rustle of small creatures in the bushes around them. It was still night, although the horizon was starting to lighten. Tato took a harder look around, Lasair flaring his flames to provide

additional light, both ensuring that the woods were safe for Sansa. When Tato was certain she would be safe, the large troll got down on one knee in front of Sansa and leaned in to give her a big hug. Lasair stood nearby, his flames smaller and darker, his eyes sad as he watched his oldest friend say goodbye to his newest friend.

"I love you Tato." Sansa whispered into his ear. Tato finally released her, stood up, and turned to Lasair. They both approached the tree again, stepping back into the shining doorway. At the last moment, Tato stopped and turned, smiling at his friend - his Princess.

"I love you too. We will wait for the other magical girls, and for Princess Sansa to return." He stepped back and the light narrowed as though behind a closing door.

Too quickly, the clearing was dark, any trace of light from the magical tree gone. The light in the sky continued to brighten, and Sansa knew she needed to hurry home. She placed her hand on the trunk of the tree one last time, feeling the tingle and seeing a momentary shimmer in the air around her.

"I will see you again. I promise." Sansa whispered to the tree before turning away and heading home.

The walk home seemed long and the woods seemed empty without her friend. As she reached the creek near Tato's home, she walked upstream so she could cross by the mine entrance he had called home. She was surprised to see that the foliage that covered the mine was gone. She stepped in, wishing she would see a fire smoldering in the fire pit, or Tato sitting in a broken lawn chair reading to Lasair. Instead, it was cold and empty. She took one last look around, then continued on her way home.

Sansa quickly reached the house, silently opening the front door and tiptoeing upstairs. Her grandparents must have still been asleep, as the house was silent and no one rushed to her when she climbed the steps. She quickly changed into pajamas, washing her face and hands in the bathroom before hiding her dirty clothes in the bottom of her suitcase and crawling into bed. She closed her eyes and quickly fell into a deep, dreamless sleep. A few hours later, there was a knock on Sansa's door.

"Time to get up, Sansa!" Lita called out.

Sansa stretched and rubbed her eyes.

"I'll be right down, Lita!" She called back.

Sansa quickly dressed and hurried downstairs. She joined her grandparents in the kitchen, and they enjoyed a nice breakfast together. They spent the rest of the day in the house, cleaning, baking, and playing games. Sansa had fleeting moments of sadness when she thought of Tato being gone, but they were quickly replaced with feelings of excitement. She couldn't wait to tell her sisters about what had happened, and about Tato. She also knew that she would see him again, and couldn't wait to return to the Fae Realm.

Time passed quickly, and after another few peaceful days with her Papo and Lita, Sansa knew her parents and sisters would be coming home. Sansa sat on the deck, waiting for their car and thinking about her adventures over the past two weeks. As she looked around the woods surrounding the house, Sansa saw a bright flash of color. She jumped up, squinting against the bright light shining from above. The flashing color flew straight at her, and Sansa knew it was Tato's friend, the hummingbird. She smiled at the little bird.

"He's gone back home."

The hummingbird flitted back and forth a few times before flying towards the road, then heading back into the woods. Sansa's eyes followed the path the beautiful bird took, waving goodbye to it as it disappeared into the shadows of the forest. That's when she heard the sound of tires crunching on the gravel. She turned back and saw her parent's car heading up the hill. Sansa took another look over her shoulder at the woods, smiled, and whispered into the wind...

"I will see you soon, my friend."

EPILOGUE

AFTER **SANSA'S PARENTS** parked, the doors to the back seat flew open, and both Bella and Katie jumped out and ran towards Sansa. The three hugged, all trying to talk at the same time. Lita came over and hugged them all, laughing.

"Girls! Everyone take a breath and let's go inside so you can take turns telling us about your adventures!"

The girls ran inside, Papo and Lita following them, their parents coming in behind. They all sat in the living room, listening attentively as each girl talked about their trip. After they had each shared their stories, Sansa asked if her parents were going to stay a little longer. Papo smiled at her before turning to the girls' parents.

"I do have a couple of steaks I could throw on the barbeque, if you'd like to stay for supper." As their parents looked at each other, all three girls started clamoring to stay. Finally, their parents laughed, and as their mom shook her head, smiling softly, their dad told them they could play outside for a while, until it was time to eat.

After everyone put on their shoes, the girls raced outside, and down the steps of the front deck. They paused, unsure of what to do, or where to go. Sansa told them both about the tree house their Papo started for them.

"He didn't get it finished yet, but I'll show you where he's building it! And then I'll take you somewhere...um, magical." Sansa whispered the last word, looking around cautiously. She missed the brief expressions of surprise that swept across her sister's faces..

Katie and Bella followed Sansa to the large tree that was becoming the home of their tree house. Papo had started building the foundation, but there was still a lot of wood and tools around the base of the trunk. As Sansa described some of the designs Papo was thinking about, the girls looked around the woods, imaging what it would look like when it was finished.

"Now, come on. Before we have to go in to eat!!" Having shown her sisters the treehouse, Sansa was now impatient to show them the magical tree. Bella and Katie glanced at each other, chuckling. They both knew how impatient Sansa could be. As if reading their thoughts, Sansa took a deep breath and tried again.

"Did you have any more questions or anything else you'd like to see? If not, I have a super cool place I'd like to show you..."

"Alright, let's go!" Katie smiled and nodded in the direction Sansa was pointing. Sansa gave her sister a big grin before turning and jogging off into the trees.

The three girls made their way through the woods, slowing down when the brush thickened. They quickly came to the creek near Tato's former home. Sansa glanced sadly upstream, before showing Bella and Katie where she had almost fallen into the water, then leading them carefully across the creek - how Tato had shown her.

Once again, they began to jog through the woods, heading towards the field where the magical tree stood, Sansa in the lead. As they burst from the trees, Sansa stumbled to a stop, frozen in shock. Where the large tree had stood, there was now only a burnt husk. Tears flooded Sansa's eyes and ran down her cheeks.

"Noooooooo...." Sansa fell to her knees, sobbing, as her sisters knelt down on either side of her. They tried comforting her but had no idea what was wrong. Sansa looked at her sisters, tears still overflowing.

"That... the burnt...." Sansa took a deep breath, then tried to explain what had truly happened to her in the woods. A few hiccups punctuated her tale, and a few times, Sansa had to take a moment to continue.

The three girls sat together on the grass, tears running down their cheeks as they listened to Sansa. When she was done, the trio stood, took hold of each other's hands, and approached what remained of the tree. When they stood at the base of the tree, light began to shimmer around the sisters. What remained of the tree crumbled to dust, leaving a bare patch of dirt in the center. A small breeze picked up, blowing some debris from inside the circle. The sun then glinted off something still half buried in the earth. The three girls knelt down, Katie brushing the dirt off what appeared to be an amulet. As Katie gently lifted the talisman from it's bed of ash and earth, she realized it wasn't one charm, but three. They came apart in her hands, one for each of the girls. The three looked at each other in shock, but then Sansa noticed something else in the earth - a small sprout of green. She grinned, knowing that this was an offshoot of the tree. One day, this small green sapling would grow into another majestic tree, possibly allowing travel back to the Fae realm. As the girls shared Sansa's hope, Bella began to tell her tale about what really happened in Canada. When she finished, she looked at her sisters and took a deep breath.

"I'd like you to call me Rex, ok? I'm Rex now."

Both girls hugged Rex before taking each other's hands. They stood together, looking out over the rolling hills as they each got lost in their memories of the past two weeks and imagining what the future would bring.

GLOSSARY

King Aneirin (A-Nee-Rin) - The last King of the Light Fae and descended from the *Tuatha Dé Danann*, beings of great beauty and grace.

Aos Si (Ees Shee) - An ancient term for the Fae races.

Cu-Sith (Coo Sith) - A large, and magical, canine that can grow to be the size of a bull.

Dragonkin - Humanoid beings who are descended from great and powerful Dragons.

Duende (Doo-En-Day) - Goblin-like creatures who delight in causing mischief.

Fae (Fay) - A collection of peoples who resemble creatures of lore and myth.

Faeling (Fay-Ling) - Smaller Fae beings who are often seen as pets to the larger Fae races.

Lasair (La-Say-Ir) - A Hearth Faeling, also known as a Fire Faeling, and friend of Tato.

Lita (Lee-Tah) - Sansa's grandmother. Lita is short for abuelita, which means "granny" in Spanish.

Maelona (May-Low-Na) - The last Princess of the Light Fae. She fell in love with a coachmen's son in Victorian England and chose to forsake her birthright.

An Tuar Ceatha (Ahn Too-as Kay-th) - Translated as "Rainbow Falls", the traditional territory of Tato's family of Light-Born Trolls.

Norn - Ancient Fae beings who can see a person's destiny and fate.

Papo (Pah-Pu) - Sansa's grandfather. Sansa could not say Papa when she was learning to speak, and instead said "Papo". The name stuck.

Sansa (Sah-N-Sa) - One of the Children of the *Aos Si*, and a very special little girl.

Tanrawdtatoeraswyn (Tan-Raw-Tah-Toe-Rahs-Win) - Also known as Raswyn or Tato. He is a Light-Born Forest Troll whose family has served the Royal House of De' Danann for centuries. He was a boyhood friend of King Aneirin and the only one the King could trust to fulfill his last wish.

ABOUT THE AUTHOR

Samantha lives in Northern California and works in the finance industry when she is not writing about fairies, princesses, and magical places. She loves reading and spending time with her family, especially her pit bull, Freyja.

WHO ARE TERRAN EMPIRE PUBLISHING AND RAINBOW UNICORN PUBLICATIONS?

Based in Northern California, USA, Terran Empire Publishing was founded in 2016 and specializes in fantasy and science fiction game products and books. Rainbow Unicorn Publications was founded shortly after to focus on products for a younger audience. With over 40 years of gaming and writing experience, the team at Terran Empire Publishing and Rainbow Unicorn Publications promise to bring creative and unique takes on genre classics, as well as new material for gamers and readers of all ages.

OTHER TITLES FROM TERRAN EMPIRE PUBLISHING AND RAINBOW UNICORN PUBLICATIONS

Stories of Norse Gods and Heroes (ISBN 978-0-9990108-2-2)
Faithful Fairy Friends (ISBN 978-0-9990108-0-8)